## *Hello Freedom!*

In the clear afternoon, the campus of Sweet Valley University looked even prettier and more perfect than it did in the colorful brochures. From the sun-dappled tree-lined streets, to the beautiful red-tiled buildings, to the groups of students laughing and talking as they strolled across the lawns, everything about the campus seemed to say, "Welcome to college. Welcome to freedom."

"We made it!" Jessica shouted as she followed Todd's BMW through the gates of Sweet Valley University. She sounded the horn. "Hello, freedom, here I come!"

Elizabeth felt a ripple of excitement herself. Her sister was right—they had made it! They really had! They weren't little kids anymore. They were college freshmen, adults in the real world.

Bantam Books in the Sweet Valley University series
Ask your bookseller for the books you have missed

#1 COLLEGE GIRLS
#2 LOVE, LIES, AND JESSICA WAKEFIELD
#3 WHAT YOUR PARENTS DON'T KNOW . . .
#4 ANYTHING FOR LOVE
#5 A MARRIED WOMAN
#6 THE LOVE OF HER LIFE
#7 GOOD-BYE TO LOVE
#8 HOME FOR CHRISTMAS
#9 SORORITY SCANDAL
#10 NO MEANS NO
#11 TAKE BACK THE NIGHT
#12 COLLEGE CRUISE
#13 SS HEARTBREAK
#14 SHIPBOARD WEDDING
#15 BEHIND CLOSED DOORS
#16 THE OTHER WOMAN
#17 DEADLY ATTRACTION
#18 BILLIE'S SECRET
#19 BROKEN PROMISES, SHATTERED DREAMS

And don't miss these
Sweet Valley University Thriller Editions:
#1 WANTED FOR MURDER
#2 HE'S WATCHING YOU
#3 KISS OF THE VAMPIRE
#4 THE HOUSE OF DEATH

SWEET VALLEY UNIVERSITY

# College Girls

Written by
Laurie John

Created by
FRANCINE PASCAL

BANTAM BOOKS
NEW YORK • TORONTO • LONDON • SYDNEY • AUCKLAND

*For Molly Jessica W. Wenk*

RL 6, age 12 and up

COLLEGE GIRLS

*A Bantam Book / October 1993*

*Sweet Valley University™ is a trademark of Francine Pascal*
*Conceived by Francine Pascal*
*Produced by Daniel Weiss Associates, Inc.*
*33 West 17th Street*
*New York, NY 10011*



ISBN: 0-553-56308-4

*Published simultaneously in the United States and Canada*

*Bantam Books are published by Bantam Books, a division of Bantam Doubleday Dell Publishing Group, Inc. Its trademark, consisting of the words "Bantam Books" and the portrayal of a rooster, is Registered in U.S. Patent and Trademark Office and in other countries. Marca Registrada. Bantam Books, 1540 Broadway, New York, New York 10036.*

PRINTED IN THE UNITED STATES OF AMERICA

OPM 20 19 18 17 16 15 14 13 12

# Chapter One

"Look at that!" Elizabeth Wakefield had been dreamily staring up at the sky, her head on Todd Wilkins's shoulder, her long, golden-blond hair falling onto his chest. She sat up and pointed through the windshield of the BMW at the brilliant light streaking through the night sky. "It's a shooting star!"

Todd squeezed her hand. "The perfect ending to a perfect night."

Elizabeth smiled. "It is perfect." There was no doubt in her mind that this was one of the most important nights of her life. Tonight she and Todd were celebrating their "last date." They'd gone to all their favorite places, beginning with a romantic dinner at the Box Tree Café and ending with a milk shake with the old crowd at the Dairi Burger.

*Old crowd.* Elizabeth repeated the phrase in her head. It was hard to believe. After four happy and successful years, she had really graduated from Sweet Valley High. She was no longer just a high school kid; she was eighteen and about to start her freshman year of college. About to leave home and all the things that were familiar to her.

That's why she and Todd had planned this night. It might not be the last time they ever went to the movies in Sweet Valley, or drove through the hills outside of town, or tossed a coin to see if they were going to go to Guido's for a pizza or to the Dairi Burger for fries. They'd be back home for vacations and summers. But it was the last night of their old life. Soon there would be new places, new friends, and new experiences.

"Who knows where we'll be a month from now," Todd said, as though reading her thoughts.

A slightly troubled look came into Elizabeth's eyes. She hadn't wanted to admit it to herself, but she was feeling the unfamiliar tingle of fear. Starting a new life meant leaving behind the things she loved.

"Are you scared?" she asked quietly.

"Scared?" Todd put his arm around her waist and held her close. "What is there to be scared of?"

"I don't know," she whispered. "It's just that when I try to picture my life somewhere else—without my mom and dad and our house and everything . . ." Her voice trailed off. *All I can see is a dark, empty space,* she finished silently.

Todd took her hand in his. "Don't think about

what's ending. Think about what's beginning. Besides, it's not like you're going to college in Alaska, Liz. Not everything's going to change. After all, you'll still have Jessica to drive you crazy."

At the mention of her twin sister, Elizabeth started to laugh with relief. Todd was right. There were some things that would never change. Flighty, frivolous, scheming Jessica would be at Sweet Valley University too. Where would Elizabeth be without her?

They were the famous Wakefield twins. Identical on the outside, opposite on the inside. Of course, they'd changed some over the years. Their hair was longer, they'd grown a little taller, and according to most people, even more beautiful.

But Elizabeth was still responsible and hard-working. She'd graduated with honors and a special award for her work on the school newspaper. She still preferred hanging out with Todd or her best friend, Enid Rollins, to partying.

And Jessica was still . . . Jessica. If there was a party in Sweet Valley, Jessica was at it; if there was a cute guy around, Jessica was after him. Jessica was still charming and stubborn and always got exactly what she wanted.

"Of course you're right," Elizabeth said. "After a week of sharing a room with Jess, I'll probably wish I *had* gone to school in Alaska."

Todd's laughter was warm and reassuring. "And let's not forget the most important thing." He pushed a long strand of yellow hair away from her face. "You'll still have me, you know."

Elizabeth snuggled against him. Todd was one of the most important things in her life. They were going to have an incredible year together. And, Elizabeth reminded herself, she'd still have dependable, wonderful Enid, too. What could she possibly be worried about?

"Just wait," Todd said. "No more rules. Nobody telling us what to do. We're about to have the time of our lives." He bent his head close to hers. "We're about to start really living."

"I don't know when we're supposed to go to classes," Elizabeth said to Enid, looking up from the Sweet Valley University bulletin. "It looks like every minute of the day is crammed with other things to do. Sorority events, clubs, parties, tryouts, dances . . . I'm exhausted just reading about it all."

"That's fine with me," said Jessica from behind the fashion magazine she was reading. "Personally, I don't see how they can expect us to fit in boring junk like science and English when there are so many more important things to do."

"I just hope I still find time to keep up my journalism," Elizabeth continued, ignoring her sister. "SVU has a great TV station. Only, I don't want my grades to suffer."

"You don't have to worry, Liz," Enid said

earnestly. "I'm sure you'll be able to do both, just like you always have."

Jessica groaned inwardly. Here she was, about to begin one of the most important and exciting times of her life, and she was surrounded by the Deadly Duo, Elizabeth and Enid, two of the dullest people in Southern California.

She stared hopelessly at the smiling model in the magazine. She really wished that her best friend, Lila Fowler, were there with her now! Lila worried about stuff that really counted, like having the right clothes and meeting gorgeous men.

But unfortunately Lila had gone to Europe for the summer and hadn't come back. She was supposed to have returned last week, but all Jessica had heard so far was from a postcard of some old church in Venice that said simply and mysteriously, "Slight delay. I'll call soon."

"Oh, give me a break, will you?" Jessica demanded, her face appearing over the top of the magazine. "We haven't even gotten there yet, and already you're moaning about your grade-point average."

Elizabeth rolled her eyes. "Not all of us are going to college just so we can buy a new wardrobe," she teased. "Some of us are hoping to get an education."

"Who cares about books when there's a whole campus full of boys to learn about?" Jessica replied.

"It's a good thing I know you're joking, Jessica Wakefield," Mrs. Wakefield said pointedly, coming over to the kitchen table and setting the coffeepot in the center. She sat down beside Enid. "There's Butler Hall," she said, pointing to a photograph in the bulletin of a pretty brick building surrounded by trees. "I used to have a lot of classes there." She turned the page. "And look, there's La Palma Drive. Look how it's changed! There used to be only a few old houses there and now it's all built up."

"Now they have electricity and running water, too," Jessica joked.

Mrs. Wakefield ignored her. "You know, I really envy you girls. Some of the best years of my life were spent on that campus. I hope you enjoy your college days half as much as I did."

Enid turned to her. "You belonged to a sorority, didn't you, Mrs. Wakefield?"

"Belonged to a sorority!" Elizabeth gave her mother a mischievous smile. "My mother was only president of Theta Alpha Theta—the most elite sorority on the entire campus."

Mrs. Wakefield nodded. "The Thetas were wonderful," she said, her eyes sparkling. "We had the best time. It was like having a ready-made family. Girls who shared your values and goals, and who were always ready to help you out . . ." Her voice trailed off as she stared out the window, lost in her memories.

Enid smiled. "I'm convinced," she said emphatically. "I'm definitely going to pledge a sorority. I'm sure it's the best way to find the right crowd."

Jessica peered over her magazine at Enid, one perfect eyebrow raised in surprise. If Lila were there and not stuck in a gondola somewhere in Venice, she and Jessica would have been laughing hysterically by now. The idea of Enid Rollins, the biggest drip since the invention of water, wanting to belong to the "in" group was too funny for words.

"The right crowd?" Elizabeth said with a smile. Jessica could tell Elizabeth found the idea as bizarre as she did. "I don't think I've ever heard you talk about the 'right crowd' before. Getting in with the right crowd is a Jessica Wakefield concept."

"But we're going to be in college now, Liz," Enid argued. "I don't want to do what I've always done. I want to change. I want things to be different." Her green eyes flashed. "I've made a big decision this summer. In high school I just let things happen to me. In college *I'm* going to decide what happens." She looked from Elizabeth to Mrs. Wakefield and back again, a smile lighting up her face. "To begin with, I'm changing my image."

Jessica couldn't contain her laughter for another second.

"Changing your image?" Elizabeth demanded. "But why? There's nothing wrong with your image, Enid. You're great as you are."

Mrs. Wakefield started pouring the coffee. "Enid does have a point," she said. "One of the most wonderful things about the next four years is having the opportunity to explore and grow."

"I couldn't agree with you more, Mom!" Jessica cut in enthusiastically. "I'm already thinking of myself as the Christopher Columbus of Sweet Valley University, exploring the new, uncharted world of sophisticated college men."

Her mother turned to her. "You, young lady, could do with a little less exploring and a little more growing."

Elizabeth put a hand on Enid's arm. "How are you going to change your image? You're not going to pierce your nose or anything, are you?"

Enid looked at her and laughed.

"There's nothing outrageous about experimenting a little," Mrs. Wakefield said. "You're allowed to do things like that when you're eighteen." She smiled to herself. "My first semester in college, I grew my hair long and dyed it black."

Jessica dropped her magazine and gazed at her mother in surprise. "That's great!" she cried. "Were you a hippie, Mom?"

"A real radical," her mother murmured.

"So, Enid, what are you planning to do?" Elizabeth persisted.

Enid sat up a little straighter, her eyes darting around the table. "Do you really want to know?"

Jessica ducked behind her magazine again. "Oh, yeah," she muttered. "Make my day."

"I'm changing my name!"

"Changing your name?" Elizabeth cried. "To *what*?"

Enid scowled at her. "To Genghis Khan," she said sourly. She put down her mug heavily. "What do you think, Liz? That I was just going to make something up? I'm going to use my middle name, Alexandra. I think it's a lot cooler than Enid."

"Even Genghis Khan is cooler than Enid," Jessica commented.

"Alexandra is a lovely name," Alice Wakefield said, lifting her own mug to her lips. "It's very sophisticated."

Enid smiled. "Thanks. I think so too."

Elizabeth was still staring at Enid in disbelief. "Since when are you so worried about being sophisticated?"

"Since I really started thinking about what I wanted out of college," Enid said.

"But—"

Jessica cut her off. "Face it, Liz," she advised. "The times they are a-changin'."

"But do they have to change so fast?" Elizabeth said, more to herself than anyone else.

Elizabeth looked at her watch. In less than an hour, Todd, Winston Egbert, and Enid, alias Alexandra, would all be pulling up in front of the house for the two-hour drive across sprawling Sweet Valley County to Sweet Valley University. Although they were each bringing a car, they'd decided it would be more fun to convoy. "Sort of like a wagon train," Winston had joked.

"Except nobody will be shooting at us."

Elizabeth picked up two small framed photographs, taken at a beach party when they were all high school juniors. In the first, she and Todd had their arms around each other and were laughing hysterically. In the second, she was between Todd and Jessica, and the three of them were grinning happily.

Elizabeth could remember the exact moment they had been taken as though it were yesterday. They'd been playing volleyball when suddenly the boys, who were ten points behind, decided it would be more fun to drag the girls into the water than continue losing. Todd had come charging under the net, scooped her up, and raced to the ocean with her in his arms. Jessica had raced after them with the camera. "I can't believe it!" she'd been screaming. "Liz and Todd are having a spontaneous moment!"

Elizabeth had planned to leave the snapshots behind, waiting on her dresser for her return at Thanksgiving, but remembering how the three of them had laughed that day, she changed her mind and laid them carefully on top of the box on the bed.

Elizabeth looked around the room once more. There were so many memories here that part of her wished she could just fold the whole thing up and put it in her trunk.

"You're being ridiculous," she scolded herself. "You'll be back in a few months."

But her eyes filled with tears at the sight of the worn koala bear and blue lop-eared rabbit sitting abandoned on her half-empty bookshelf. Jessica had laughed at her when she'd tried to pack them. "We're going to college, not nursery school!" Jessica had said. "You can bring a basic black dress and a linen suit with you, but you cannot bring a blue bunny."

Elizabeth gave herself a shake. Thinking of her sister reminded her that they'd better finish loading the Jeep.

She turned toward the bathroom connecting her room with her sister's. "Jessica!" she called. "Are you almost ready?"

Elizabeth came to a sudden stop in the doorway. Her sister's room didn't look heartbreakingly empty as hers did. It looked messier and more cluttered than it had when she started packing.

"Jessica, what are you doing?"

Jessica looked up from the floor, the picture of innocence. "I'm packing. What does it look like?"

Elizabeth put her hands on her hips. "It looks like you're digging for the ruins of an ancient temple." Her eyes scanned the room, from the small mountains of clothes on the floor to the boxes spilling over with papers and books. She gave an exaggerated sigh. "You have got to be the only person in the world who can pack for two weeks and still end up with more junk than you started with."

Jessica's sea-green eyes flashed indignantly. She

scooped up another armload of shoes and dumped them into her purple canvas bag.

"Maybe all *you* need are some notebooks and a few pens." She went back to her closet and removed a few more laden hangers. "But *I'm* going to have an adventure." She held up a long dress patterned in red and gold. "Isn't this great? These are *the* colors of the season." She smiled mischievously. "After all, a girl does have to dress for adventure. You can't leave these things to chance."

Elizabeth eyed the stunning red-and-gold dress, with its tight bodice and low-cut back. Like most of the clothes that were heaped around the room, it was new in more ways than one. Jessica had never owned clothes so obviously sophisticated before. Apparently Alexandra Rollins wasn't the only person changing her image this autumn.

"Well, I'm planning to have an adventure too," Elizabeth said, a little defensively. "I'm not going to just stay in our room and study, you know."

Jessica threw the season's colors on top of her suitcase, turning back to her twin with a serious expression. "Can we get one thing straight right now, Liz?"

"Sure," Elizabeth said, a little surprised by her sister's tone. "What is it?"

Jessica frowned. "I don't want you pulling your 'I'm the big sister' routine on me anymore. I've agreed to share a room with you, but not if you're going to act like you're my mother. I don't want you nagging me about cleaning up. I don't want you asking me where I've been or when I'm coming back. And I definitely don't want you telling me who I can date."

Elizabeth opened her mouth to answer, but nothing came out. Jessica made it sound as though she were doing Elizabeth a favor by sharing a room with her.

"I have no intention of telling you *whom* you can date," Elizabeth finally managed to squeak. "But if you think you can keep *our* room the way you keep this dump—"

"You see? I knew it!" Jessica tossed back her head, her eyes blazing. "I knew you were going to get on my case the first chance you had."

"Me? I didn't get on your case. You're the one who—"

"I'm not going to take it, Liz, I mean it." Jessica folded her arms, her cheeks flushed. "For eighteen years all I've ever heard is how you're four minutes older than I am, like it's some big deal or something. Like it gives you the right to boss me around. Well, I don't care if you're forty years older than I am! Now that we're in college, I'm going to do exactly what I want!"

Elizabeth had to laugh. "Since when have you ever done anything else?"

"Me?" Jessica's voice was shrill with indignation. "Are you accusing me of being self-centered, Elizabeth Wakefield? *You?*"

Elizabeth stared at her sister in disbelief. Where had Jessica been for the past eighteen years? There wasn't a person who knew her who hadn't accused her of being self-centered at one time or another. Aristotle believed that the earth was the center of the universe, Aristarchus believed that the sun was the center of the universe, and Jessica Wakefield believed that the center of the universe was Jessica Wakefield.

"What do you mean, *you*?" Elizabeth raged. "Are you suggesting that *I'm* the one who's self-centered?"

Jessica marched over to the closet and yanked out another clump of skirts and blouses. "Oh, no, not *you*," she sneered. "Not Princess Perfect, the Girl Who Can Do No Wrong." She started pulling the clothes from their hangers and stuffing them into her bag. "You've been bossing me around since we were little. But we're adults now, Liz, and I'm really not going to take it anymore!"

"Well, don't!" Elizabeth yelled back. "See if I care!"

*It's a good thing we know we're adults now,* Elizabeth thought as she stormed back to her own room, *because we sure sound like kids.*

"Well, that's that," Mr. Wakefield said as the last suitcase was finally wedged into the back of the Jeep. He slammed the rear door and turned to his daughters with a smile.

Jessica groaned inwardly. The smile on Ned Wakefield's face was one of his embarrassed I-Am-Your-Father smiles. This meant that he had a little farewell speech he'd been preparing. Much as she loved her father, Jessica had never been a fan of his serious talks.

Jessica looked down Calico Drive, hoping to be rescued by the sight of Winston's beat-up old Beetle or even Todd's BMW turning the corner. There was nothing coming.

Mr. Wakefield cleared his throat. "Well . . ." he said again. "This is a day your mother and I have been planning for since you two were born."

Jessica turned back to him with a grin. "You mean finally getting us out of the house?"

Mr. Wakefield laughed. "No, of course not," he said, moving forward and putting an arm around each of his daughters. "You know how much we're going to miss you. The house is going to seem very empty . . ."

"We're going to miss you and Mom, too, Dad," Elizabeth said.

Ned Wakefield coughed, giving them each a squeeze. "I just want you to know if there's anything you need, anytime . . . If you need to talk to me or your mother, if you need some advice about school . . . or boys . . . or anything like that—"

"Sure, Dad." Jessica hadn't meant it to sound sarcastic, but she wasn't exactly in a hurry to get her dad's opinion on guys.

Mr. Wakefield turned his gaze on her, a new

concern on his face. "I understand that you're very excited about all your new freedom, Jessica," he said slowly, "but with freedom comes responsibility. And being away from home doesn't mean you can run wild. Before you agree to go out with someone—whether it's a boy or even a girlfriend—I want you to ask yourself, 'What would my mother and father think of this person?' "

Jessica stared back at him with a glazed expression in her eyes. *What would my mother and father think of this person?* Some cute guy was going to ask her out and she was supposed to stop and ask herself if her father would want her to date him? As sweet as her father was, he was so completely out of touch with reality sometimes that it was a wonder he functioned at all.

Mr. Wakefield released his hold on them and folded his arms. He looked up at the few clouds lazily drifting through the sky. "Let me tell you a story," he said, smiling to himself. "I was your age once myself, believe it or not. I know how you feel. I remember when I first went away to college. I thought I was a big man. I had everything worked out. . . ."

Jessica tried to catch Elizabeth's eye, but Elizabeth was looking up at their father earnestly. Maybe Elizabeth was taking the move to college harder than Jessica had thought. Worrying about classes was one thing, but seriously listening to one of Mr. Wakefield's When I Was Your Age reminiscences was something else.

Just when Jessica feared that nothing was going to save them, the back door opened and a golden streak ran out, hurling itself at them with a happy bark.

"Prince Albert was afraid you were going to forget to say good-bye to him," Alice Wakefield said with a laugh, following him out to the driveway.

Jessica had never been so happy to see him before. She leaned down and gave him a hug. "I'm going to miss you, boy," she told him as he nuzzled against her ear. "I bet there's nobody at Sweet Valley University who can fetch a stick like you can."

Elizabeth bent down beside them, resting her head on Prince Albert's silky neck.

Jessica glanced over. Amazingly enough, there seemed to be a tear in her sister's eye. "Oh, come on, Liz," she whispered. "You're not going to start crying over the dog, are you?"

Elizabeth shook her head. "I'm not crying. I was just thinking about the first day we got him. Don't you remember how little and cute he was? Remember how he couldn't get up on our beds without help?"

"Oh, look!" Mrs. Wakefield said. "There's Todd and Alexandra."

"And Winston," Mr. Wakefield added as the putt-putt-putt of the bright orange Beetle suddenly sounded on Calico Drive.

Jessica waved as the cars drew up to the curb.

"We'll be right there!" she called, practically tripping over herself in her desire to get going. "Well, we'd better go," she said, giving her parents each a quick hug and slapping Prince Albert on the head. "Come on, Liz. We don't want to miss one minute of our new lives, do we?"

"Not one," Elizabeth mumbled.

Jessica marched past her. She was already at the Jeep when she realized that her twin wasn't behind her. Turning around, she saw Elizabeth hurling herself into Mrs. Wakefield's arms.

*Talk about long good-byes,* Jessica thought as her sister and her mother both brushed tears from their cheeks. "Come on, Liz!"

"I'm coming!" Elizabeth shouted back.

Jessica started the engine. However bizarre Elizabeth was acting, she was sure that once they were at Sweet Valley University, Elizabeth would forget all about how cute Prince Albert was when he was a puppy and she'd be fine. "The College Express is about to depart!"

Elizabeth didn't move.

Of course, it was going to be very hard for Elizabeth to settle into college life if she refused to leave the driveway.

# Chapter Two

In the clear afternoon, the campus of Sweet Valley University looked even prettier and more perfect than it did in the colorful brochures. From the sun-dappled tree-lined streets, to the beautiful red-tiled buildings, to the groups of students laughing and talking as they strolled across the lawns, everything about the campus seemed to say, "Welcome to college. Welcome to freedom."

"We made it!" Jessica shouted as she followed Todd's BMW through the gates of Sweet Valley University. She sounded the horn. "Hello, freedom, here I come!"

Elizabeth felt an unexpected ripple of excitement herself. Her sister was right—they had made it! They really had! They weren't little kids anymore. They weren't just visiting their brother, Steven. This was where they lived now. They were college freshmen, adults in the real world.

"I love it, I love it, I love it!" Jessica screamed. "I really do." She gestured out the window. "Look at it, Liz! Isn't it beautiful?"

Elizabeth looked. Although it was the beginning of freshman orientation and classes wouldn't start for another week, it looked as though the entire student body had already arrived for a week of fun. And Jessica was right, it was beautiful. Suddenly her anxieties of the past few days seemed foolish. She felt as though she'd been in one of those troubled nights when you lie awake worrying about everything. Elizabeth sighed with relief. Arriving at Sweet Valley U was like waking up to find the sun streaming through the window and her problems no more than phantoms of the night.

She smiled happily as she gazed out the window. She could see herself walking down the steps of the library. She could see herself sitting on one of the wooden benches along the pathways, reading a book. She could imagine throwing a Frisbee on the lawn with Todd. Elizabeth's confidence began to return. She'd been worried about nothing. College was going to be great.

"This is definitely the place to be," Jessica said, heading toward Dickenson Hall, their new home. "I mean, will you look at that, Liz? Just look over there."

Elizabeth turned. "Oh, wow! That's the new art and drama complex. They must have finished it over the summer. Doesn't it look great?"

Jessica groaned. "My sister, the android. I point out one of the cutest boys I've ever seen, and all you see is a dumb building." She shook her head. "Maybe you're not ready for college after all."

Dickenson Hall was a modern, multistoried dorm with a lush, green expanse of grass in front and a parking lot behind. Its halls were filled with talk and laughter, and scores of girls and their friends and families carrying everything from leather suitcases to life-size cardboard cutouts of James Dean.

Elizabeth took a bag from the Jeep and followed Jessica and their brother, Steven, into the large white building that was now her home. All the noise and activity were reassuring. Everyone they passed said hello.

Jessica looked over her shoulder at her. "Isn't this cool?" she asked, her blue-green eyes almost glowing with excitement. "It looks just like one of those singles apartment complexes you see in movies. All it needs is a pool."

"And all you need is a mule," Steven Wakefield groaned as he staggered up the stairs ahead of them with Jessica's trunk. Like the good brother he was, Steven had agreed to meet the twins outside their dorm to help them unload the Jeep. "I don't understand why you have so much stuff." He banged against a wall. "When I first came here, I had two suitcases and a box of books."

"That's because you're a boy," Jessica said,

coming up behind him. "Boys are simpler creatures. Their needs are fewer."

"My needs are going to include a new back after this," Steven said. He dropped the trunk on the landing and collapsed on top of it. "What have you got in here, your bathtub?"

"Clothes," Jessica said, sailing past him with a box of tapes in her arms.

"Clothes?" Steven stared after her. "What kind of clothes? Armor?"

"Clothes for every conceivable occasion from afternoon tea to a midnight scuba-diving party," Elizabeth said. She put a comforting hand on his shoulder. "She wanted to hire a moving truck, you know, but Dad put his foot down."

Steven watched Jessica make her way down the corridor, searching for room 28. "When is she going to have any time for classes?" he asked. "She's going to be changing her clothes from morning to night."

Elizabeth laughed. "I'm not sure Jess realizes she has to go to any classes."

"Hey, you two!" Jessica called from the other end of the hall. "Here's our room!"

"You better hope it's bigger than my first college room," Steven said as he got back to his feet. "Or with all the stuff Jess has, you'll be sleeping in the hall."

*And I thought Dickenson Hall was noisy,* Elizabeth thought as her eyes scanned the campus snack room for her best friend. The place was packed with people, most of them shouting to be heard above the jukebox blaring music from the corner.

"Where are you, Enid?" she mumbled, her eyes darting from table to table. Even though everyone she'd met so far seemed very friendly, the newness of the place was a little overwhelming. Suddenly she felt as though a dozen people were looking at her, and she forced herself to smile as though she knew what she was doing.

She was just about to give up and wait for Enid outside when she saw someone waving from across the room. Elizabeth's heart jumped with relief. Enid had already changed into an outfit Elizabeth had never seen before, but it was definitely her, grinning happily from the entrance to the food line.

"I can't tell you how happy I was when you called," Elizabeth said as she reached her friend. "I really needed to be rescued from that room. I can't believe Jessica abandoned me like that. Five minutes, Enid. That's exactly how long she stayed. I timed it." She took a chocolate doughnut from the snack-bar shelf. "Five minutes and she was out the door, leaving me to set up the room all by myself. I wanted to kill her."

"Alexandra, Liz, not Enid." Enid filled a cup from the coffee machine. "Or maybe Alex. Alex sounds pretty cool, doesn't it?"

The irritation Elizabeth was feeling with her sister transferred itself to her friend. "Enid, Alexandra, Alex, Lucretia Borgia, who cares?" she snapped. "I'm trying to tell you something."

In her heart, Elizabeth knew that she was overreacting, but she wanted some sympathy. She'd assumed that Steven was going to spend some time with them since it was their first day, but after they unloaded the Jeep he'd made some excuse and went back to his off-campus apartment. *Well, at least I've got Jess,* Elizabeth had told herself.

But Jessica stayed just long enough to grab the bed by the window and half of Elizabeth's closet, and then raced off in search of fun.

Enid dropped a container of yogurt on her tray. "I care, Elizabeth," she said shortly, moving toward the cashier. "But you're not telling me anything that I haven't heard a million times before, and the truth is, I'm getting pretty tired of hearing it." She reached into her bag for her wallet. "So Jessica's acting like a spoiled brat and leaving you to do all the work. So what else is new?"

Feeling slightly stunned, Elizabeth watched Alexandra Rollins pay for her coffee and yogurt and then scan the snack bar for a table. How could somebody change so quickly? Elizabeth and Enid had been best friends for years, and in all that time Enid had always been sympathetic and supportive. She had never hidden the fact that she thought Jessica was a spoiled brat, but she'd also never come out and said so in so many words. Not in that tone of voice.

"Let's sit over there." Enid gestured toward a table in the center of the room and then, not waiting for Elizabeth's answer, strode over to it.

Elizabeth fumbled in her pocket for change. And Enid had never sounded quite so snotty with her before. It wasn't as if Elizabeth was the annoying member of the Wakefield family. She was the Wakefield twin everybody loved.

Her eyes followed Enid as she crossed the snack bar. Not only was her personality changing, but she seemed to be walking differently too: slower, more deliberately. Frown lines appeared on Elizabeth's forehead. Alexandra was wearing an outfit that Enid wouldn't have been caught dead in—tight jeans and a form-fitting bodysuit.

"Are you planning to pay for that or are you just going to stand there staring into space?"

Elizabeth turned around. The woman at the register was glaring at her unpleasantly.

"You're holding up the line," she said.

Elizabeth glanced behind her. Several unsmiling students were standing there, waiting impatiently. One of them had actually started eating his sandwich.

Elizabeth felt her cheeks turn red. "Oh, of course . . . I—I'm sorry . . ." She pulled out a handful of coins. In her haste to hand them over, several spilled from her grasp. They sounded to Elizabeth like firecrackers going off as they landed on the linoleum floor. No one made a move to help her pick them up. She bent down, scrabbling around people's feet to retrieve the dimes and pennies.

"Your change is on the tray," the cashier snarled.

The line moved forward. The guy behind her, under whose heel Elizabeth had spotted a nickel, stepped over her.

*Forget the money,* Elizabeth told herself. *Just get your stuff and get out of here.* She stood up so quickly that the next girl in the line slammed into her. Elizabeth picked up her tray. Coffee had sloshed all over, making a small pool on which her doughnut sat like an inner tube on a lake.

"Freshmen," said the cashier as Elizabeth fled. "It's the same thing every year."

"At last," Winston Egbert said as he pulled the VW into the parking lot outside Oakley Hall. "I was beginning to think this place didn't exist."

Once the Sweet Valley convoy had entered the college grounds, the girls had gone off to find their rooms and Todd had headed to the special high rise that housed the varsity athletes, leaving Winston to find his dorm by himself. Only, he hadn't been able to find it. Most of the male dorms were grouped near one another, but though he'd driven around in circles for half an hour, from building to building, he hadn't been able to find Oakley Hall. Finally, seeing a very pretty young woman who looked as though she knew her way around, Winston stopped and asked.

"Oakley?" she said, giving him an almost conspiratorial smile. "Sure, it's right over there. Third on the left."

And there it was, third on the left, set down in the middle of the female dorms like a rooster in a flock of chickens. *This must be my lucky day,* Winston thought as two attractive girls in shorts and tank tops sauntered past the Beetle.

One of them slapped the bumper. "Cute car," she said in a loud, clear voice.

"Isn't it great?" the other one said.

Winston beamed. And he'd been worried that the Beetle might interfere with the sophisticated, worldly, man-about-campus image he was hoping to create for himself. He checked himself in the rearview mirror. The new hairstyle was still in place. The Ray Bans he'd squandered a large chunk of his graduation money on still looked cool. He gave himself a wicked, worldly grin. Yes, this was clearly his lucky day.

Whistling to himself, he climbed out of the car, hauling a leather carryall—another large chunk of his graduation money—and a box of books out of the back. Several more girls walked by, all of them giving the Volkswagen and its owner warm looks. *I have the feeling I'm really going to enjoy college life,* he thought happily.

By the time he'd located his wing and his hallway, Winston's mood had begun to dim slightly. He had the uneasy feeling that something was wrong. The corridor was crowded with people who were looking for their rooms. Already, music blared from several doorways and there was a lot of loud talk and laughter. The funny thing was, though, that every voice he heard, and every person he saw, was female.

*I must have made a mistake,* Winston thought. *I must be in the wrong wing or something.*

He lifted his sunglasses and looked up at the sign on the wall. *Wing B—Rooms 11–20.* He looked at the letter in his hand. He'd been given room 18, in wing B, which was supposed to be made up of small, single rooms. He checked the letter again. Yes, that was what it said: wing B, room 18. And it was definitely in Oakley Hall.

Winston smiled self-consciously as another group of girls struggled past him, their arms filled with boxes. They all smiled back. He saw hair dryers and makeup mirrors, curling irons and coffee machines. These girls were not visiting; they were moving in.

*It must be a coed dorm,* he decided. Relief engulfed him. That would explain it. It was a coed dorm, the guys were already in their rooms, and he had somehow gotten himself on the wrong floor.

Winston took a deep breath and sidled down the hallway, trying to appear as inconspicuous as possible. He glanced into each room out of the corner of his eye. There was a redheaded girl in number 12 who waved as he passed. There were three girls sitting on the single bed in number 16, drinking sodas and talking. They all looked up as he passed. "Are you lost?" one of them called to him.

Winston froze. "Me?" *Please don't let them know I was a clown in high school,* he silently prayed. *Please don't let me blush, please don't let me stammer, and please don't let me smile like Daffy Duck.*

The girl in the middle, who had the longest legs he had ever seen on anyone who wasn't a professional basketball player, laughed. Her laugh was nothing like a professional basketball player's. Her laugh was pure crystal. Winston felt his solar plexus beginning to dissolve.

"No," she said, "that guy behind you." She laughed again. "Who are you looking for? I'm the resident assistant for this floor, Maia Stillwater. Maybe I can help you."

An RA, that was just what he needed. By not breathing he managed to keep his voice steady. "My name's Winston Egbert,. And maybe you can help me." He took a step forward, but because the dark glasses made indoor visibility poor, he misjudged the doorway, and instead of striding forward in a commanding, masculine way he crashed into the frame and catapulted himself into the room.

There was a creaking of springs as the three attractive young women collapsed on the bed in hysterical laughter.

"Are you okay?" Maia gasped.

Winston could feel the new, cool Winston Egbert wobbling and Winston the clown trying to take over. "Yes, yes," he said quickly. "I'm fine. I must have tripped over something." He gave himself a shake, and hanging on to as much dignity as he could, completed his journey into the room.

"This is Candy Fierro," Maia said, nodding to the girl on her right. "And this is Anoushka Koll." The two of them were still laughing.

"Hi," said Winston, deciding that he could forgive them because of Candy's almost-purple eyes and Anoushka's heart-melting smile.

"So what's the problem?" Maia prompted. "You can't find your girlfriend?"

Winston tore his attention away from those eyes and that smile. "Well, no. Actually the problem is that I can't find my room."

The three girls exchanged a glance.

"Here?" Maia sounded incredulous.

"Well, I thought it was here." Winston handed her the letter. "I guess I must've made some kind of mistake or something."

Candy and Anoushka leaned over Maia's shoulder while she read. "This is Oakley Hall," Candy said.

"And this is wing B," Anoushka said.

Maia looked up. "And room eighteen is right next door." She grinned. Her smile was not quite up to Anoushka's, but close. "There aren't any men living here, though. It's strictly women." She read the letter again. "I don't get it. How could they have made a mistake like this?"

Suddenly Candy started laughing again. "Look!" she cried, stabbing at the paper with a daggerlike metallic-pink nail. "Look, there's what happened. The computer got your name wrong."

Maia and Anoushka started laughing too.

Winston sat down beside Candy, looking at the top of the letter where her finger was pointing.

"Oh, I don't believe this," he groaned. He must have read the letter at least ten times, and somehow he'd never noticed its first, basic mistake. *Dear Winnie Egbert,* the letter began.

Candy put an arm around him. "Cheer up, Winnie," she said. "I'll let you borrow my electric curlers anytime you want."

"You coming with us, Todd?"

Todd shut the dresser drawer he'd been filling with clothes and turned around. He'd spent so much time getting introduced to the other guys on his floor that he'd just started to unpack.

Bryan Mars, captain of the basketball team, was standing in the doorway of Todd's room. Behind him, several of the other team members were talking and fooling around.

"Where are you going?" Todd asked.

Mark Gathers, the team's undisputed star, poked his head over Bryan's shoulder. "We're going to this great Cajun diner a couple of miles up the road. You've got to come, Todd. You haven't lived till you've tried their red beans and cornbread."

Todd stared back, suddenly confused. They couldn't be going for dinner yet? He felt as if he'd just gotten here. "What time is it?"

Bryan looked at his watch. "It's seven, amigo. Chow time."

*Seven!* Todd couldn't believe it. Only a little while ago it was four o'clock and he was going to ride over to Dickenson Hall and look for Elizabeth. But another bunch of guys had arrived, and they'd all started talking, and then a couple of the other guys had gone off to unpack and that had seemed like a good idea . . .

"We don't want to stay out too late tonight," one of the other freshmen said. "We have to get up early to take advantage of priority registration."

Todd hesitated, looking at the grins on the faces of Bryan and Mark. They were great guys. He really wanted to hang out with them some more. And red beans and cornbread sounded pretty good, too. But what about Elizabeth? She was probably expecting to eat with him tonight.

"Come on, Todd!" someone else shouted. "We haven't told you the end of the story about the game with U of O yet. You're going to lose it when you hear what Murgatroyd did."

On the other hand, Elizabeth had Jessica—*and* Steven. Steven was helping them move in; he'd probably planned to take the twins back to his place for dinner. Todd didn't have to feel guilty about Elizabeth. She was fine. She was the one who should feel guilty about him. It hadn't even occurred to her to invite him to dinner with Steven. And besides, Todd really wanted to hear what Murgatroyd had done.

"Okay," Todd said, reaching for his jacket. "Sounds great."

As they all piled into the elevator, it crossed Todd's mind that he could give Elizabeth a ring from downstairs. Just to make sure she was at Steven's and that everything had gone all right. But as they came into the lobby, Mark Gathers caught up with him.

"There's no reason for all of us to take cars," he said. "Why don't you come with me and I can fill you in on all the things you really need to know about life at SVU?" He smiled. "Like which sororities have the fastest women."

Todd wasn't sure if Mark was joking or not, but he didn't want Mark to think he wasn't sophisticated enough to be interested in fast women. After all, he was a college man now, and already a prized member of the basketball team that had been state champion four years running.

Todd smiled back. "Why don't I drive so you can concentrate on talking."

As she walked toward the campus coffee bar,

Jessica couldn't help thinking how lucky she was. She'd been at Sweet Valley University for only a few fantastic hours, and already she'd made friends with Isabella Ricci, one of the most popular and stupendous sophomores on campus. Jessica couldn't help smiling to herself as she strutted across the lawn. She'd been missing Lila a lot the last few days. Not just because she was concerned about Lila's whereabouts, but because though Elizabeth had Todd and Enid to talk to, Jessica didn't really have anyone to share her own excitement with. Now she had Isabella Ricci. Isabella was even more beautiful and sophisticated than Lila. And she knew *everybody* who was anybody and had dated almost every eligible man on campus.

Jessica caught sight of the clock tower at the end of the quad. It was almost six thirty. She'd promised Isabella she'd meet her at six thirty to hear a jazz trio playing in the café this evening.

Jessica was running as she came up the path that circled the café, but as soon as she turned the corner, she slowed down. When she walked through the doors of the café, it was with the step of a woman who has seen it all. She stopped just inside the entrance. She kept her expression slightly bored, but inside she was bubbling with enthusiasm. Dark and cramped, with posters and paintings on its brick walls, the café looked like something out of a French movie. The students sitting at the candlelit wooden tables, all of them nearly as sophisticated as Isabella, were talking in low, intimate voices and drinking coffee from small white cups. *You can have your gondola, Lila,* Jessica thought. *I'd much rather be here.*

As casually as she could, she looked around the room. Thank God, the trio hadn't set up yet. She would have died of mortification if she'd had to walk through them while they were playing.

Jessica shook her head, and her golden hair shimmered in the subdued light. She didn't have to look to know that she was creating a sensation. She'd spent the whole afternoon practicing making an entrance, imitating the way she'd seen Isabella walk and stand and gaze around a room, and so far it hadn't let her down once. She could feel the eyes sizing her up: the girls with envy, the guys with admiration.

At a table in the corner she saw the long white neck and tousled black hair of Isabella Ricci against the red wall of the coffee bar. She looked as though she must be thinking of something incredibly romantic. In high school Jessica would have waved, but not now. Now she was a college woman. She raised her head ever so slightly, just enough to let Isabella know that she'd seen her, and crossed the coffee bar like a model walking down a catwalk, like Isabella Ricci crossing a street.

Jessica had heard of people who went through their entire lives without ever understanding why they'd been born. There always seemed to be people in TV dramas and the kind of books they made you read in English who had no idea what their lives were about. They spent hours or hundreds of pages trudging around being miserable and wondering why their lives had no meaning. But not Jessica. She might be only eighteen, but she knew exactly why she'd been put on this earth.

So she could go to college.

There wasn't a doubt in her mind. Today had been the most wonderful day of her entire life. This was where she belonged. This was where she was meant to be. In only a few brief hours, she had not only met scores of people and made an incredible new friend but she'd been asked out by not one, not two, but four different men.

Jessica reached Isabella's table and slid into the empty seat with a sigh. "I'm sorry I'm late," she apologized. "I wanted to put my name down on the tryout list for cheerleading, and I had trouble getting out of the gym."

Isabella looked concerned. "Did you get lost?"

Jessica smiled. "No, I mean, these adorable guys kept stopping me, wanting to talk."

Isabella threw back her head and laughed. "Jessica Wakefield, you really are too much. I thought I was the only wild woman on this campus, but obviously I was wrong." Her gray eyes sparkled with mischief. "You are definitely a girl after my own heart."

"We were destined to meet," Jessica said. "If I

hadn't bumped into you in the gym, I would have bumped into you somewhere else."

One perfect Ricci eyebrow rose a fraction of an inch. "Speaking of which," Isabella said, barely seeming to move her lips, "don't look now, but there's someone headed toward us who looks as though he'd like to do more than bump into you."

Jessica kept her eyes on Isabella. "Who is it?" she asked. "Somebody I should know?"

"Somebody everybody should know." Isabella lifted her cappuccino to her lips and took a small, delicate sip. "Peter Hazlitt Wilbourne the Third, president of the Sigmas and the most powerful undergraduate on campus." A smile flickered over her lips but didn't land. "Peter thinks he's God's gift to earth. Some people think he's the gift of someone else entirely."

"Now I really am interested," Jessica whispered. "Where is he? Can I turn around now?"

Isabella raised her eyes. "Why, Peter," she purred. "How nice to see you. You're looking very well after your summer vacation."

Peter stopped beside Jessica. "I didn't come for chitchat with you, Izzy, and you know it," he said dismissively. "I wanted to be introduced to your little friend."

Isabella made a face. "Don't mind Peter, Jessica," she said with mock sweetness. "Rudeness is part of his charm." She waved an arm at Jessica and her gold jewelry flashed. "Jessica Wakefield, Peter

Wilbourne the Third. Peter, Jessica."

Jessica turned around to find herself looking at one of the most arrogant, self-satisfied faces she'd ever seen. It was also an undeniably handsome face, but not half as handsome as its owner seemed to think.

"Well, how do you do?" he asked, but in such a way that Jessica knew he was really saying, *Aren't you lucky to get to meet me?*

Jessica returned his insincere smile with one of her own. "How do you do?"

He leaned closer. "You know, I don't usually go out with freshmen," he said in a smooth, smug voice. "But I think in your case I might make an exception." He reached out and touched a strand of her hair. "How about going to one of the house parties with me this week? I'm pretty busy with frat stuff for the next night or two, but the Sigmas are having a party with the Thetas at their house on Friday that might interest a girl like you."

Jessica smiled sweetly. "I'm sorry," she said, her voice almost as smooth and smug as his, "but I've already got a date for the Theta party."

He ran a finger up her arm. "Break it."

Jessica's smile didn't falter. "I'm afraid I can't."

Peter looked over at Isabella. "Didn't you tell your little friend who I am?" he asked. "Doesn't she know there's no one on this campus who can't be dumped for me?"

"She told me who you are," Jessica said. "But I don't believe in breaking dates."

Isabella shook her head as Peter strode back to his table. "I'm not so sure you should have done that," she said. "Peter's a bad enemy to have. Some people even think he's the leader of a secret society on campus. You know, all very heavy and power obsessed."

Jessica shrugged. "I don't care what he leads. I really do have a date with this gorgeous guy I met at lunch."

"I just hope he's worth it," Isabella said. She lifted a tiny spoonful of froth and coffee to her lips. "What's this Prince Charming's name?"

"Danny," Jessica answered. "Danny Wyatt."

The spoon stopped inches from Isabella's blood-red lips. *"Danny Wyatt?"* she repeated. "But Jessica, Danny Wyatt's—"

"I did notice that he's black, if that's what you were going to say," Jessica cut in. She was a little taken aback that someone as worldly and intelligent as Isabella should feel it necessary to point this out to her.

"There's that, too," Isabella said slowly. "Hey, don't get me wrong," she rushed on, seeing the look on Jessica's face. "I'm not saying he's not a terrific guy, because he is. Everybody knows that. Danny's great. But everybody also knows that Peter Wilbourne is not a really big fan of interracial couples." She bit her bottom lip. "Seriously, Jess.

Peter has this thing about Danny. Up until last year, he and Danny were in constant competition, and Danny always won. Peter was used to being number one because he's rich. But Danny was smarter, he was stronger, he was better looking, he was nicer and more popular—he would probably have been president of the Sigmas, too, if he hadn't dropped out last winter. Peter will go nuts when he finds out he's been iced in favor of Danny. Peter hates him, Jess. I mean, really hates him."

Jessica leaned back as the trio came onto the small, makeshift stage. "Well, maybe he won't find out who I turned him down for."

Isabella smiled grimly. "Oh, he'll find out."

Outside room 28, Dickenson Hall was full of talk and music. Inside room 28, the only audible sound was the ticking of Elizabeth's watch.

Elizabeth, sitting on her bed with her hands folded on her lap, glanced at herself in the mirror on the back of the closet door. She knew that anyone who saw her sitting there would assume that she was about to go out to have a good time. Her hair was back in a loose French braid, she was wearing her favorite cranberry linen dress, and her bag and her jacket were on the bed beside her. Elizabeth scowled at her reflection.

"Well, they'd be wrong," she said out loud. "I'm not going anywhere. I'm all dressed up with nowhere to go."

For at least the twentieth time in the last forty minutes, her eyes turned to the intercom on the wall by the door. She couldn't bear to look at her watch again.

Laughter like gunshots echoed down the hallway. As far as she could tell, everyone who wasn't out at some special event on campus or in town was having a party in the dorm.

*Probably everyone in the world but me is either out having a good time or throwing a party,* she thought bitterly. *A party I'm not invited to.* She dared a quick look at her watch. It was nine. Nine! That meant she'd been sitting here, waiting for nothing, for two whole hours. Elizabeth picked up the book she'd been trying unsuccessfully to read and threw it across the room.

She'd thought that after their coffee she and Enid would probably do something together. There was a free film showing in the movie house on campus, and she'd seen a poster for jazz at the coffee bar, but Enid had other plans. "Gee, I'm sorry, Liz," she'd said. "I just assumed you and Jessica and Todd would be seeing Steven tonight, so I told some of the girls on my floor that I'd go for pizza with them."

But Jessica never came back to the room, and Todd had disappeared too. When Elizabeth came back to the dorm and couldn't reach him on the phone, she'd been sure he must be on his way to pick her up. She'd been so sure, in fact, that she'd gotten dressed and gone to wait in the lobby for him. She'd waited until she got tired of people looking at her as though she were in the wrong place, and then she'd come back to her room.

One of the girls on her hall had asked her if she wanted to go to the campus pub, and a couple of other girls had invited her to the common room to watch a movie, but Elizabeth still thought Todd would show up and she didn't want to miss him.

"Well, I shouldn't have worried," she said to the empty room as she kicked off her shoes. "I could have gone to San Francisco and he wouldn't have noticed."

She lay back on her bed, imagining her parents at home, reading together in the living room. "I wonder what the girls are doing right now," her mother was probably saying. Her father would laugh. "Oh, you know them," he'd say. "Wherever they are, they'll be having a good time."

Down the hallway, several people started laughing as though they'd just heard the funniest story in the world.

But in room 28, Dickenson Hall, it was just about then that the tears began to fall.

# Chapter Three

Elizabeth rolled over in her sleep, kicking off the covers. "Jessica!" she moaned. "Please let me in!"

Elizabeth was lost in the dark, bare concrete corridor of an enormous dorm. For some reason she was wearing her pink-and-white-striped pajamas and her hair was in pigtails. On her feet were blue bunny slippers; in her hand was the suitcase she'd had as a child. She couldn't find her room.

Scared and lonely, Elizabeth wandered up and down a maze of hallways. "Excuse me," Elizabeth kept saying. "Excuse me, but I'm looking for my room."

They laughed. "Oh, it can't be in this dorm," they told her. "You're just a little kid."

She began knocking on doors. Every room was filled with laughing, happy students, dressed in fashionable clothes and sipping champagne.

Growing desperate, Elizabeth shuffled along, trying to keep anyone from noticing the tears streaming down her cheeks. And then, down at the end of a dimly lit corridor, she saw it: number 28, her room!

Through the open door she could see her beautiful sister, stretched out on a chaise longue, a crystal goblet in her hand and her head thrown back in a laugh. Jessica was wearing a red-and-gold brocaded cocktail dress, and her hair was piled on top of her head. She was surrounded by handsome men, kneeling in a circle around her.

And then Elizabeth's eyes fell on what was behind Jessica and the men. It was her old room on Calico Drive, and all her things were just as they should be. Overcome with joy, Elizabeth moved forward.

But at that instant, Jessica turned and saw her. "No!" she screamed. "You can't come in here! You'll ruin everything."

Tripping over the bunnies' ears, Elizabeth started to run. She had to get inside; her room was there, her *old* room, her real room. Once she got inside, everything would be all right again. Just as she reached the door Jessica slammed it in her face.

Crying uncontrollably now, Elizabeth started pounding on the door. "Jessica!" she called. "Jessica, let me in!"

Suddenly Elizabeth's eyes blinked open. She sat up in bed, her heart pounding. *It was just a dream,* she told herself, trying to calm her breathing.

She looked around. The sun was streaming

through the blinds, illuminating the piles of clothes on the floor, the half-unpacked suitcases, the stacks of boxes. Socks and underwear dripped off the furniture, and curtains sat in a heap on top of Jessica's dresser, waiting to be hung. A purple lace bra hung over Elizabeth's brass desk lamp.

Elizabeth swung her legs over the side of the bed. Despite the chaos around her, for the first time in the two days that she'd been at Sweet Valley University, Elizabeth was actually relieved to be in room 28.

Her eyes fell on the other bed, and a feeling of annoyance started creeping back. Jessica, in her new satin purple nightshirt, was still sound asleep. The clothes she'd been wearing last night lay in a pile on the floor, just as she'd stepped out of them. Jessica was smiling.

*I'm not going to lose my temper,* Elizabeth told herself as she climbed out of bed. *I'm going to be calm. I'm going to be reasonable and understanding.* She calmly picked up her sister's jacket and hung it on the back of a chair. *You see?* she said to the pale face that stared back at her from the mirror on the closet door. *You don't have to get upset. Everything's going to be fine.*

Elizabeth wasn't sure how it had happened, but in just two days, she and her twin had driven each other to the brink of insanity. Yesterday morning, Elizabeth had accused Jessica of being irresponsible, and Jessica had accused Elizabeth of being as much fun as wet socks. "You must've been asleep by *ten* last night!" Jessica had raged. "Old people go to bed at ten, Liz, not college freshmen. You better hope you die young, because you're not going to have anything to look forward to when you retire." And then she'd stormed out of the room and Elizabeth hadn't seen her again. Until now.

Elizabeth wanted to start all over. She had given it a lot of thought, and she'd decided that it was up to her to be more flexible. To give things a little time to settle down.

After all, it had worked with Todd. Instead of giving him a hard time because he'd abandoned her the day they arrived, she'd acted as though nothing had happened. She hadn't told him how she waited for him that first night, or how she'd cried herself to sleep. And things between them were almost back to normal. Yesterday they'd had a nice dinner before he had to go off to some basketball meeting. And today they were getting together for breakfast and to register for classes.

Elizabeth smoothed out the spread and stood up, smiling to herself. Jessica had done a lot of running around in the last two days, but by now she was probably ready to get down to hanging the curtains and putting away her luggage.

Taking a deep breath, Elizabeth went over to Jessica and gave her a shake. "Hey, sleepyhead," she whispered. "You better get up. We have a lot to do today. We've got to finish setting up the room. We have to register for classes. And we have to start buying our books. . . ."

Jessica rolled over, pulling the covers over her eyes. "Books?" she mumbled. "Are you kidding? I don't have time for books. I have two teas and a lunch date today. I have to get my sleep."

"Well, maybe if you hadn't stayed out till four in the morning, you'd have already had your sleep," Elizabeth answered, a little less patiently and understandingly than she'd intended.

Jessica groaned. "Oh, don't start."

"I'm not starting," Elizabeth said calmly. "I just meant that if you actually spent a little time here, you'd be able to unpack. You could even put some of your stuff away."

"I don't want to put my stuff away," came the muffled reply. "I'm too busy right now."

Elizabeth could feel her calm vanishing as she stared down at her sister's purple sheets. It wasn't fair that she always had to be the one who was flexible while Jessica did exactly what she pleased.

"You're not too busy right now," Elizabeth snapped. "Now's the perfect time to discover two wonderful inventions—drawers and closets. You'd be amazed how handy they are. They completely eliminate the problem of having to step over dirty bras and socks to get to the door. Not only that," she rushed on, "but there is a luggage room, you know. We don't have to keep your suitcases and your trunk in here for the rest of the year."

Jessica pulled the pillow over her head. "I wish we didn't have to keep *you* in here for the rest of the year."

"Come on, Candy, hurry up, will you? If I don't get a move on, I'm going to be late for registration."

"Has anybody seen my green bra? You know, the shiny support one? I think maybe I dropped it in the bathroom last night."

"What about you, Maia, do you shave or wax? I'm always cutting myself. On the other hand, though, I really hate the sound when you rip the hair off your legs."

"Can somebody lend me a tampon? It's an emergency."

"Men! Can you believe that cretin? He broke our date *again*!"

Hurtling out of sleep like a rabbit being smoked out of its hole, single words registered in Winston's brain. Wax. Bra. Tampon. Cretin. His first thought was: *Where am I*?

And then he remembered. He was in Oakley Hall, room 18, surrounded by girls.

Very, very slowly, Winston opened his eyes.

"Anoushka! Winnie said I could borrow his weights after you, so don't forget to give them to me before you go out."

And closed them again. His free weights. Winston had thought that suave college men were all into weights, but it was beginning to look as though it was college women. He hadn't seen his since he'd dropped them on his foot as he was bringing his stuff in from the car, and Anoushka had pounced on them like a cat on a bug. He should have left them home. He should have left himself home with them.

After two hectic days of running around from office to office trying to get the computer to admit it had made a mistake when it put him in a women's dorm, Winston was exhausted. And defeated. He had eventually found a human in the office of the dean of students who conceded that something had gone radically wrong.

"I know it's an unusual situation," Ms. Lombardi had sympathized, "but I'm afraid you're stuck with it, Mr. Egbert, at least for the time being."

"Stuck with it?" Winston had repeated. "What do you mean, stuck with it?"

Ms. Lombardi had smiled, more wryly than sympathetically. "I mean, like Super Glue. You may not have been aware of it before, but there's a severe housing crisis at the university, and I'm afraid there isn't a spare bed in any of the male or coed halls at the moment. Not even off campus."

"But I can't be stuck with it," Winston had protested. "I'm a b— I'm a man. I can't live in a hall filled with girls."

"You mean women," Ms. Lombardi had corrected him. "And I'm afraid that unless you'd prefer to sleep in your car, you're going to have to live with them until things settle down. Once a few people start dropping out or moving into the frat houses we'll be able to find you a place."

"But Ms. Lombardi . . ." Winston had leaned forward so that the other women in the office wouldn't overhear him. "You have no idea what it's like. They never stop talking. And they walk around in their . . . in . . ." It had been difficult to say the words out loud, especially when halfway through his sentence he'd realized that Ms. Lombardi, despite the fact that she must be at least forty, was a woman too.

Ms. Lombardi's lips had twitched, as though she were about to start laughing. "They run around in their *what*?"

"In their underwear! How am I supposed not to look? It's very embarrassing. I have to wait till they're all done in the bathroom, and even then I have to brush my teeth with my eyes closed in case one of them's still in the shower. Plus, I have to be dressed all the time . . ."

Her lips had twitched again. "Winston, trust me," she'd said. "You'll get used to it. After all, you're a college man now, right? I'm sure you'll handle this just fine."

The corridor had gone silent. Winston opened his eyes again.

Even if he did handle it just fine, he still had a

problem that he hadn't been able to explain to Ms. Lombardi. He was hoping to impress the frat guys with what a big man he was. What were they going to say when they found out he was living with a bunch of girls? A bunch of girls who called him Winnie and borrowed his weights?

Winston listened. He glanced at the clock. They stopped serving breakfast in half an hour. That explained it—they'd all gone to talk about tampons and men over scrambled eggs and cornflakes. Pulling on his jeans and a T-shirt, Winston warily stuck his head out the door. He looked left. He looked right. The coast was clear.

*Please,* he hoped as he dashed into the bathroom. *Please don't let there be anyone in here waxing her legs.*

Elizabeth's stomach growled, and she didn't blame it. She felt like growling herself. She'd been waiting nearly half an hour for Todd, and he still hadn't shown up. If he didn't hurry, the kitchen would be closed. She forced herself to look away from the door. *Three more people,* she told herself. *If Todd isn't one of them, then I'm going down to breakfast by myself and wait at the table.*

The one real advantage to being one of the last students to come for breakfast was that there wasn't any line. Elizabeth walked right up to the counter and put some fruit and cereal on her tray. Then it occurred to her to take some extra for

Todd, in case he didn't get there before the kitchen closed. She took a glass of juice, a doughnut, and a bagel with cream cheese for Todd. She also got the hot dish for Todd and an order of toast for herself. She was going to need her strength for registration, and besides, from the horror stories she'd heard, she probably wouldn't be done in time for lunch. She smiled to herself as she had her meal ticket punched. From what she'd heard, she'd be lucky to be done by dinner.

Elizabeth decided to sit in the middle of the cafeteria so Todd would see her as soon as he came in. Several girls from her dorm waved as she made her way across the room. She was smiling back at Daria Mendez, with whom she'd struck up a conversation in the bathroom last night over the cold-water faucet that wouldn't go off, when she felt someone staring at her from a nearby table. Thinking that it might be Todd , she turned—only to find herself staring into the ice-blue eyes of a boy she didn't know. His gaze was so intense that she bumped into another table in confusion.

Where *was* Todd when she needed him? Elizabeth grabbed the first empty table she came to, throwing herself into a chair with a sigh of relief.

That was another thing about college life she hadn't counted on, that other guys might start coming on to her. At Sweet Valley High everyone knew that she and Todd were a couple. But here it seemed as if every time she turned around, some guy was staring at her as though he'd never seen a girl before in his life.

Elizabeth munched on her apple while she waited for Todd. She was really looking forward to seeing him. He'd been so excited yesterday about the basketball team and all the great guys on it that she'd barely had a chance to tell him anything she'd been doing. Not that she'd been doing much. Hanging around, waiting for Jessica to turn up. Hanging around, waiting for Todd.

She tossed the apple core on her tray and started putting butter and jam on her toast.

She hadn't been doing *nothing* for the past two days. She'd talked to a bunch of girls in her hall yesterday. She'd visited the library and the arts complex, and she'd signed up for both the school paper and the news department of the campus TV station. In the evening, she'd made popcorn and nachos with a couple of people from her floor and watched an old movie. If she hadn't been thinking about Todd most of the evening, wondering where he was and if he was missing her or not, she might have actually enjoyed herself.

Elizabeth checked her watch. She lifted the plate covering Todd's breakfast. The eggs looked a little solid, but the potatoes were still warm. She broke a piece off with a fork. She might as well eat the hash browns. There was no use in letting the whole meal go to waste. Not when there were so many hungry people in the world.

Elizabeth reached in her bag and took out the registration handbook. That was the other thing she'd done yesterday. She'd spent hours combing through the course listings, picking out what she wanted and fitting it all into a workable schedule. She was excited about the result. Not everything might be going right for her at the moment, but she was looking forward to some really interesting classes. After all, that was what college was about. Even if Jessica didn't think so.

Elizabeth made a sandwich out of a piece of toast and some cold scrambled egg. She ate it slowly while she went through her schedule again. Because she'd taken advanced history and English in high school, she was able to go straight to the courses she really wanted: a creative-writing workshop, a literature course on the roots of feminism, a foundation course in classical thought and culture, the social history of the twentieth century, and Journalism I.

Elizabeth put down Todd's juice glass with a happy sigh. She was going to have to do a lot of reading, but it was going to be worth it.

"Liz!"

Elizabeth looked up. Todd had just burst through the doors and was hurrying toward her.

"Liz, I'm sorry," he was saying even before he reached her. "I'm really, really sorry."

He looked really sorry. He was probably so exhausted from all the basketball practice that he'd overslept. "It's all right, Todd," she said with a smile.

He smiled back and gave her a kiss. "You're the best, Liz." He flung himself into the chair beside her. "I completely forgot all about meeting you because of registration."

"Registration? What do you mean?"

"You have freshman burnout already?" he teased, tapping the leaflet she'd been reading. "Registration for classes, remember?"

Elizabeth stared at him. "But you couldn't have registered," she finally managed to choke out. She picked up her listing of course offerings and shook it in his face. "Freshmen whose names begin with W don't register until eleven."

Todd winked in a disgustingly supercilious way. He must have picked it up in the athletes' dorm, because he had never winked like that before.

"They do if they're on a varsity team," he said.

"Oh, do they?"

"That's right. They get to preregister before registration even begins."

Impossibly enough, his smile was even more supercilious than his wink. No wonder he had no time for her. He was too busy taking lessons in how to be a superjock.

"It was so cool, Liz. We didn't have to wait in line or anything. We just told them what we wanted, and they punched it into the computer."

Elizabeth shoved the tray away from her. "But

we were going to register together."

"I know," he said, not quite meeting her eyes. "I would've called you before I went this morning, but it was so early and rushed . . ." He shook his head. "I couldn't have done it anyway. I've got practice this afternoon. And then we've got a booster dinner."

He got to his feet suddenly. "Come on, Liz. Why don't we go to the snack bar and get a coffee? I have just enough time before I have to meet the rest of the guys."

"But what about your breakfast? I got extra food for you."

Todd laughed. "You really do have freshman burnout, don't you?" he teased. He pointed to the tray. "There's nothing there."

Elizabeth looked in disbelief. Todd was right: there was nothing left but a few spoonfuls of cereal and an apple core. She must have been hungrier than she'd thought.

"It's a good thing I already ate with the team," Todd said, putting his arm around her.

"Oh, right," Elizabeth said. "A very good thing."

Jessica had gotten into bed smiling, she'd smiled through her sleep, and now she woke up with a smile still on her lips. What a day she'd had yesterday! What a fabulous day! Isabella and Isabella's friend, Denise Waters, had taken Jessica on a head-to-toe tour of the campus. She'd seen the pond where the frat boys went skinny-dipping. She'd seen the window a girl had climbed out last winter when she eloped with the new history lecturer. She'd seen the lawn where Denise's friend, Mariela Winterson, punched another girl for trying to steal her boyfriend. She'd seen Isabella's tremendous double suite in the new apartment complex. She'd been asked out by five more gorgeous guys.

Jessica stretched languidly, slowly opening her eyes. Thank God, Elizabeth was gone. If there was one thing that could stop Jessica from smiling these days, it was her twin sister.

Jessica looked over at Elizabethland, her sister's side of the room, with irritation. You'd think they were in boot camp, not college. Everything in Elizabethland was neat and tidy. The bed was made. The furniture was dusted. The few things that were out—her framed photographs, her jewelry box and brush and makeup bag, the slippers under the bed—looked as though they'd been glued in place. In fact, Elizabethland was so neat that you wouldn't think anyone lived in it.

Jessica kicked off the covers and sat up. Not that anyone did live in it. Not anyone *real.* "The Stepford Twin," Jessica muttered to herself as she got out of bed.

"Oh, geez. Where's my underwear?" Jessica asked aloud. She had to have blue underwear to go with her blue-and-white flowered leggings and blue sleeveless shirt. She shuffled through another heap of clothes and looked into a couple of suitcases, but her blue underwear was gone. "I bet *she's* put it somewhere," Jessica grumbled.

Jessica yanked open the top drawer of Elizabeth's bureau. Elizabeth *always* kept her underwear in her top drawer. And there it was. Everything, even the tights, was neatly folded.

"It must be exhausting being so neat all the time," Jessica muttered. "No wonder she never has any time to have fun."

She pulled out a sky-blue pair of bikini underwear and a matching bra, grabbed her shower stuff from the top of a box, and hurried from the room—leaving Elizabeth's top drawer open, like a hole in the perfection of Elizabethland.

"I don't know how much more of the Stepford Twin I can take," Jessica said as she bit into a croissant. What could be more sophisticated than having something you could barely pronounce for breakfast? "You should have heard her shouting at me this morning. The whole hall heard her." She took a sip of the espresso coffee Isabella had made in the tiny kitchenette of her suite. Croissants *and* espresso. If Lila Fowler could see her now, she'd be so envious! "I'm telling you, I'd rather live with my mother than with Elizabeth."

Denise put down her cup. "You have my sympathy, believe me, Jess." She was one of the most beautiful girls Jessica had ever seen, but she was so unself-conscious about it that you hardly even noticed. "Last year I got stuck with this complete dork. She dressed in nothing but brown, and all she ever ate was seeds and nuts."

"Tell her about Mommy," Isabella urged, laughing.

Denise rolled her almost-black eyes. "Oh, God." She leaned toward Jessica. "I swear, Jess, every sentence that came out of this girl's mouth started with 'Mommy says . . .' *Mommy says you should never eat anything that's been processed . . . Mommy says brown is the most harmonious color . . . Mommy says young women should never raise their voices.* God, it was a nightmare!"

Jessica laughed. "You can't be serious. She couldn't have been that bad."

Isabella was shaking her head. "She was worse. She used to play this tape of crickets all the time to relax her inner self."

"By the end of the first week, I wanted to strangle her outer self," Denise said. "I still can't believe I got through an entire semester listening to bugs."

Jessica collapsed against the sofa in hysterics. "Stop it," she begged. "You're making Liz sound almost human."

Isabella nibbled delicately on her croissant. "You know, Jessica, I just may have the solution to your roommate problem."

"Really?" Jessica straightened up. "What?"

Isabella nodded toward the room. "Why don't you move in here with me? Ms. Loyola, the dorm dictator, said last night that she didn't think my roommate was going to show up after all. And they're going to have to find someone to take her place anyway . . ."

Jessica couldn't believe it. Isabella Ricci, one of the most popular girls in the whole school, provider of croissants and espresso coffee, was asking *her* to share her suite.

"I don't want to pressure you or anything, Jess," Isabella added quickly. "I know you'll need some time to think it over, but we should let Ms. Loyola know before she finds someone else . . . another nut-and-bug woman."

Denise laughed. "You should do it, Jess. Your sister will be fine. She'll probably be as relieved to get rid of you as you'll be to get away from her."

"I'm not saying I'm a perfect roommate," Isabella said. "But I'm not too hard to get along with. Am I, Denise?"

Denise smiled. "Easy as instant pudding."

This was more than she'd dared hope for. Jessica was so excited she hardly trusted herself to speak.

"What's the matter?" Isabella asked when Jessica still didn't respond. "Is something worrying you? Ask me whatever you want."

Jessica took a deep breath. "Well . . . I do have one question . . ."

Isabella held out her hands. "As the gunslinger said to the sheriff, shoot."

"When can I move in?"

*Six and a half hours. Six and a half hours, and for what?* Elizabeth fumed as she made her way back to her room. Six and a half hours to be shut out of the class she'd wanted most, Journalism I.

She staggered through the front glass doors of Dickenson Hall with a sigh. For the first time since she arrived, it actually seemed to her like a quiet and sane place.

*I'm exhausted,* she thought as she started up the stairs. *I'm emotionally and physically exhausted. What I need is some peace and quiet, a nice hot shower and a nice dinner.*

She turned down her hall. The good news was that she could have all three of those things. There was no way Jessica was going to be in the room, not at five forty-five in the evening. Jessica wouldn't be back for hours.

She stopped outside the door of her room with a puzzled frown on her face. She could hear voices inside. She looked at the number again. It was definitely her room. Something heavy hit the floor. Elizabeth was just about to reach for the knob when the door flew open and two large, good-looking young men walked past her, Jessica's trunk between them.

"What—"

But before Elizabeth could finish her sentence, a girl Elizabeth had never seen before stepped out, Jessica's purple satchel over her shoulder and a box of shoes in her arms. She looked more like a Paris model than a California college student, except that she was wearing ripped jeans and a faded Save the Rain Forests T-shirt.

"Hi," she said. "You must be Elizabeth." She stuck a hand out toward her. "I'm Denise Waters."

Stunned, Elizabeth shook the slender white hand.

"I'll meet you guys in the car," Denise called over her shoulder. She smiled at Elizabeth again as she passed her. "See you around."

As much as Elizabeth wanted to know what was going on, she was almost afraid to ask. She stepped into the room. And into another exquisite-looking girl, this one dressed in black leggings, a tight black top, and gold jewelry, who was carrying Jessica's tape deck.

"Oh, my God, you really are twins!" she exclaimed. She looked from Elizabeth to Jessica. "It's kind of creepy, isn't it? Having somebody around who looks *exactly* like you? It's like living in an episode of *The Twilight Zone*."

Elizabeth was looking at Jessica too. Jessica had two hats on her head and was leaning over Elizabeth's desk. She turned with a big smile on the face that was exactly like Elizabeth's.

"Oh, Liz, I'm so glad you showed up!" she cried. "I was just writing you a note."

*Oh? I wonder what this note was going to say,* Elizabeth thought. She decided not to speak. If she opened her mouth, she might start screaming or, worse, crying.

"Have you met Isabella?" Jessica gestured toward the other girl. "Isabella, this is my sister, Liz. Liz, Isabella Ricci."

Elizabeth continued to stare at her sister in silence. *If Jessica smiles any harder, her mouth will crack,* she thought. Jessica picked up an armload of dresses from the back of Elizabeth's chair. "Isn't it wonderful?" she asked. "Isabella's asked me to be her new roommate!"

Elizabeth dug her nails into her palm. *And I wonder if you bothered to tell her that you already had a roommate.*

Jessica started toward the door. "I would've told you before, Elizabeth, but we only just thought of it."

Isabella made a sad little face. "The girl who was supposed to share with me never turned up, so Jessica's really being a lifesaver."

Jessica came up beside Isabella. "I'll drop by tomorrow, Liz, and we can work out a schedule for the Jeep."

Elizabeth nodded blankly.

"Elizabeth . . ." Jessica took a step forward. "You're blocking our way. Isabella and I have to get going. We're meeting some people for dinner."

Elizabeth's voice was low but hard when she finally found it. "What about me?"

Jessica wrinkled her nose. "What do you mean, what about you? You weren't invited. It's Amber's birthday."

"What about me?" Elizabeth repeated. "You're just going to walk out and leave me on my own?"

"I don't see why you should be upset," Jessica said flatly. "You don't like living with me anyway." She hitched up the clothes in her arms. "And besides, you're not going to be on your own. They'll get you another roommate."

Isabella slipped past Elizabeth. "I'll meet you outside," she said.

"No, I'm coming with you!" Jessica pushed past her sister. "I don't have anything else to do here."

Elizabeth stood in the doorway, without moving or thinking, for several minutes. Jessica's voice echoed through her head. *I don't have anything else to do here. . . .*

And then, very slowly and calmly, Elizabeth walked over and sat down on her bed. And very quickly and angrily dissolved into tears.

# Chapter Four

Elizabeth told Enid about Jessica moving out as the two girls walked across the campus to a sorority open house. "I was upset at first," Elizabeth admitted as they passed beneath a tunnel of palm trees. "But then I realized that it's actually the best thing that could have happened."

Enid waved at someone across the lawn. "Oh, really?" she asked, sounding slightly distracted. "Why is that?"

Elizabeth laughed. "Because now I'll be able to share with you."

Enid came to a sudden stop. "With *me*?"

"Of course with you. Who else?"

Enid shrugged. "Liz, I already have a roommate. And Trina and I get along really well. I'm not going to leave her in the lurch now."

Elizabeth couldn't believe her ears. She'd felt such a sense of relief when she realized Jessica's leaving meant that she'd be able to room with Enid, just as they'd always planned. It hadn't occurred to her that Enid might say no.

"But Enid, you *wanted* to room with me," Elizabeth argued. "You were so disappointed when I told you I'd decided to room with Jess."

"For the hundredth time, Liz, my name is Alexandra, not Enid. I really think you could make a little effort to get it right."

Elizabeth kicked a few leaves out of her way. She was beginning to feel as though she couldn't get anything right. "I'm sorry, *Alexandra,*" she said, struggling to control her emotions. "I will try, I promise—but you did say you wanted to be my roommate. You said you'd always hoped we would room together in college."

Enid gave her an almost pitying look. "Oh, come on, Liz, that was last summer. Things are different now."

"Last summer was only a few weeks ago," Elizabeth protested. "And besides, I don't see how things are that different."

"Don't you?"

They turned toward the Pi Beta Phi house.

"No," Elizabeth said, "I don't. You're still my best friend, aren't you?"

"Of course I'm still your best friend," Enid said quickly. She kept her eyes straight ahead. "It's just that I don't want things to be the way they were in high school, that's all."

Elizabeth stopped and turned to her friend. "What do you mean?" she asked. "Weren't you happy then?"

Enid met her eyes. Her look was cautious.

"I *was* happy, Liz," she said with a sigh. "But I was also in your shadow. I was Enid Rollins, Elizabeth Wakefield's best friend."

"Oh, E— Alexandra—"

"No, it's true, Liz, and you know it. It was like you were Batman and I was Robin." She shrugged. "Your decision to room with Jess got me thinking about all this. And I decided I'm tired of being Robin. Now I have a chance just to be me, and I'm going to take it."

Elizabeth opened her mouth to say something, but there was nothing to say. Enid was right. Elizabeth had been the star in high school, and Enid had been the star's sidekick.

Enid touched her shoulder. "Come on," she said gently. "It's not the end of the world. We're still best friends. And I'll bet a little change will do you as much good as it'll do me."

Elizabeth nodded. "Um . . ." she mumbled, not really trusting herself to speak.

"Come on," said Enid, slipping her arm through Elizabeth's. "Let's go see what the Pi Beta Phis are like."

The Pi Beta Phis were not the most prestigious sorority on campus. They didn't have the most popular and wealthiest girls. None of them were models or daughters of film stars. And they certainly weren't the sorority all the "right" people wanted to join.

Pi Beta Phi was known as the sorority of eccentrics and activists. They didn't wear a sorority blazer as the other houses did. Not even today, at their get-acquainted open house. The only way you could tell the Phis from the other girls was that most of the Phis were either wearing Help the Earth Fight Back badges or AIDS ribbons or were dressed so casually that they had to be members since they obviously weren't trying to make a good impression.

Elizabeth thought they were wonderful. Unlike some of the other houses, the Pi Betas actually encouraged individualism and even a certain amount of offbeatness, which Elizabeth was starting to find very appealing.

Elizabeth took another cookie and looked around the room with a smile. Even though she was a little overdressed for the house in her glamorous new black dress, for the first time since she'd arrived on campus, she felt really relaxed. The sorority house was cozy, and the girls themselves were warm, intelligent, and interested in a wide variety of things. So far that afternoon she'd had conversations about civil rights, gothic novels, and vintage motorcycles. But even more important, she was sure that the Pi Beta Phis liked her.

"I'm taking the car, Liz. I have to go into town."

Elizabeth had spotted her sister as soon as she arrived, but Jessica was with some friends whom she hadn't made any move to introduce, so Elizabeth had ignored her, too. She'd then forgotten about her so completely that she hadn't even heard Jessica come up beside her.

"I can't wait to get out of here anyway," Jessica went on. "This place is the pits. I haven't seen this many dogs since the last time I took Prince Albert to the vet."

Elizabeth rolled her eyes. "Actually, I was just thinking how much more friendly and interesting the Pi Betas are than the usual sorority zombies," she said frostily.

"You would." Jessica made a face. "You're into saving whales and women's rights and stuff like that, but most people think it's boring." She nodded toward several Pi Betas. "I bet the most exciting thing they do is take their bottles to the recycling center."

Elizabeth could feel her temper rising. "They're a lot more exciting than the Thetas," she snapped back. "At least they have more on their minds than what people are thinking and saying about them."

Jessica was staring at her as though she'd said something outrageous. "Are you kidding?" she asked. "The Thetas are *Mom's* sorority. The Thetas are the most prestigous sorority in the whole school. Isabella and Denise are Thetas."

If Elizabeth hadn't already taken a dislike to the Thetas, learning that Isabella and Denise belonged would probably have done it.

"The Thetas are a bunch of elitist snobs," Elizabeth said. "They won't even consider taking anyone who isn't pretty and doesn't dress the way they do."

"Well, that certainly isn't a problem with the Pis." Jessica cast a meaningful glance around the room. "Half of them couldn't get a date on the planet of the apes."

"Boy, what an enlightened woman you are," Elizabeth snapped. "They have more important things to think about than getting dates." Elizabeth was having trouble keeping her voice down. "They're not afraid to be different."

"They couldn't afford to be afraid to be different," Jessica shot back. "They're barely human as it is."

Elizabeth felt like kicking her sister. "They are socially aware. They contribute to the community," she told her. "The only thing your stuck-up friends might contribute is jobs for the fashion industry."

A sudden silence fell. Every girl in the room was looking at them. Elizabeth felt the blood rush into her cheeks. She'd been shouting. She'd finally found a group she liked—girls she wanted to impress—and what did she do? She shouted at her sister like a seven-year-old.

Jessica, who didn't give a used lipstick for what the Pi Beta Phis thought of her, smiled. Elizabeth could see her sister was enjoying her discomfort.

"I have to go now," Jessica said in a sweet, calm, and very audible voice. "I have to go into town and create a few jobs for the fashion industry."

The sun was shining, the radio was playing a catchy love song, and Jessica's head was filled with images of herself, dressed in something chic and sexy, stepping over the prostrate bodies of all the boys she'd refused to date as she went off into the sunset in the arms of . . .

Jessica turned the Jeep into the main street of town. She'd met dozens of boys in the past few days, one more gorgeous than the next, but she still couldn't put a face to the man of her dreams. The handsome, intelligent face of Danny Wyatt appeared in her mind. She was going shopping for her date with him, but although she was looking forward to the evening, she already knew that Danny didn't give her that special buzz. No, now that she was beginning to realize how many great-looking guys there were in the real world—and how easy they were to get—she was determined that the man who won her heart was going to be really special. The kind of man who could dine with kings but looked gorgeous in a T-shirt and jeans. Handsome . . . charming . . . witty . . . wealthy . . . sophisticated . . .

Bang!

Jessica gripped the steering wheel. *Oh, my God, where did this guy come from? I didn't even see him!*

In front of her—very close in front of her—was a blood-red 1964 Corvette in perfect condition. That was, it had been in perfect condition up until a few seconds ago. Now its taillights and back bumper were so close to the Jeep they were sort of part of it. The Jeep, though, seemed OK.

"What are you, *blind*?"

Jessica pushed open the door of the Jeep and started to climb down. "I'm sorry," she said. "I'm really, really sorry."

He was standing between the two cars, staring at the damage, shaking his head. "You're not as sorry as you're going to be." Tearing his eyes away from the Corvette's crumpled rear, he turned to face her.

Jessica was about to say she was sorry again, but the words died in her throat. Not two feet away from her was the most drop-dead handsome man she had ever seen. He was tall and lean but muscular, with dark hair and hazel eyes that looked almost golden. He was dressed in faded black jeans, cowboy boots, and a white T-shirt. His hair was longish in front and fell over his forehead in an incredibly appealing way. She didn't think she'd seen a man this beautiful on a movie screen or in a magazine. Whoever the Corvette driver was, even angry, he exerted a powerful, charismatic charm.

"I know it's my fault," Jessica said, recovering

slightly. "And I'm really sorry, I really am. But I didn't even see you."

And he was angry. He was definitely angry.

"Didn't *see* me?" The golden eyes flashed. "How could you not see me? I was right in front of you. Right behind the stop sign. The car is *red*, Princess. Dragon's-blood red. You can see it in the dark."

Half of Jessica wanted to burst into tears, and the other half wanted to check how she looked in a mirror.

*How could I not have seen this guy?* she asked herself. Those clean, classic features . . . those sparkling eyes . . . that sensual mouth . . . that incredible car . . .

"Well, it's not as though it's a write-off or anything," she said, trying to sound more reassuring than defensive. "I'm sure the insurance will pay—"

"You bet your blind blue eyes the insurance is going to pay," he snapped back. He pointed to the small but ugly dent in the Corvette. "Do you have any idea how much bodywork costs for a car like this?" he demanded. "Do you know how hard it is to match that color?"

*Do you know how good you look in that T-shirt?* she wondered. Out loud she said, "But it's possible, right? It can be matched. And I said I'll pay . . ."

"But what if it can't be matched? What if they botch it? I've spent a fortune customizing this car. It was perfect. Flawless. And now, because you were paying no attention to where you were going, it isn't."

Horns started honking around them.

"But it can be fixed!" Jessica wailed.

Why was he giving her such a hard time? She'd said she was sorry, she'd agreed to pay; what more could she do?

"But it might not be the same," he argued. "It may never be perfect again."

The honking grew louder. Jessica glanced around. They were causing a mini traffic jam. Pretty soon she wasn't going to have just one man mad at her, but dozens.

"Look," she said, "I'll give you my name and everything, and we can straighten this all out later." She reached into her bag and pulled out a notebook and a pen. "All right?"

"All right. Don't forget your phone number."

"I won't forget my phone number." She looked up, holding out the sheet of paper. And that was when she realized that besides the thick dark hair and golden eyes, he had a smile that could melt a polar ice cap.

"Don't think for one minute that this is the end of it," he said. He snatched the paper from her hand. "You'll be seeing me."

Jessica watched him walk away from her. She had to stop herself from shouting after him, *When?*

Winston sat back against the wall, smiling happily to himself. For the first time in days he was surrounded not by young females talking about premenstrual tension, but by young males talking about football. He was really enjoying himself. He hadn't felt this normal in days.

The first person Winston ran into when he arrived at the joint Sigma-Theta rush party was Bruce Patman. Bruce had been a year ahead of Winston at Sweet Valley High and never exactly a close buddy, but tonight they'd greeted each other like twins who had been separated in childhood. Bruce was pretty big in the Sigmas. He'd put his arm around Winston's shoulders and introduced him to all his frat brothers as "My friend, Winston, one of the funniest guys I know."

Winston smiled again. Here he was, sitting on the stairs with a couple of Sigmas, listening to the exploits of past rush weeks, being called Winston, and having a wonderful time. The Sigmas were definitely cool. There was nothing flaky or clownish about them; they had character and style. One of the juniors even had a Volkswagen Beetle a year older than Winston's. "It's about time we had another Bug in the Sigmas," he'd said.

Winston took a pretzel from the bowl on the step below. He was having no trouble picturing himself in the blue Sigma jacket, sitting on these very stairs next year, telling funny stories about his own rush week.

A Sigma named Gary was telling him about the camping trip they went on in the spring.

"It's great, Winston," he said. "We do the whole

thing: tents, wood fire, mountain climbing, white-water rafting . . ."

"Oh, listen to macho man," one of the other Sigmas said, laughing. "Gary's the guy who got treed by a wolf last year."

"A wolf?" Winston asked. "Where'd you go camping?"

The Sigmas all started laughing hysterically.

"It was a wolf named George who was with his owners in the next campsite," one of them gasped.

Gary grinned. "All right, all right, so I overreacted. But it was dark. German shepherds look a lot like wolves in the dark."

Winston was joining in the laughter when he suddenly saw something in the doorway that wiped the smile from his lips. Candy, Anoushka, and Samantha Holtzman, a girl from the floor below, were just coming into the house.

Panic grabbed Winston's heart. *Oh, man, what if they see me?* he thought. *What if they call me Winnie?* Any chance he had of being pledged to the Sigmas would be out the window. Guys who went white-water rafting weren't going to take the mascot of a girls' dorm seriously. He got up so quickly he knocked over the pretzels. "Bathroom," he mumbled, already rushing up the stairs. He was pretty sure there was a back staircase that led into the kitchen. He could get out the back door.

*And if there isn't a back staircase?* he asked himself as he reached the safety of the second floor. He knew the girls were near the stairs, because he could hear Candy's giggle. *Then I'll jump off the roof.*

Elizabeth nibbled on a potato chip, also wondering whether the Theta house had a back door. This was the worst party she'd ever been to. She didn't like the crowd. She didn't like the music. She didn't like the atmosphere. The only thing that met her approval was the refreshments. Even the Thetas couldn't ruin pretzels and potato chips.

Elizabeth shifted her position, trying not to look as alone as she was. Although she'd come to the Sigma-Theta party with Alexandra and some girls from Alexandra's floor, they had quickly abandoned her in favor of hanging out with a group of Thetas and their dates. Elizabeth could have gone with them if she had wanted to hear another conversation about the number of rooms in Peter Wilbourne's beach house.

"What's wrong with you, Liz?" Enid had demanded when Elizabeth had declined to join them. "Theta's *the* sorority on campus. And anyway, I thought it was your mom's sorority."

*I never in my life thought I would hear Enid Rollins sound so much like Jessica Wakefield,* Elizabeth said to herself.

"I don't feel that comfortable with them," she'd answered. Another time, she might have made more of an effort to fit in, but she didn't feel like it tonight.

All her life she'd been at the center of everything—beautiful and popular and part of the crowd—and it had been effortless. Now she was discovering what it felt like to be an outsider.

Elizabeth reached for another potato chip. It was awful. It was like being in a country where you couldn't speak the language. The funny thing was, though, that tonight she didn't really care. The feeling of dislike she'd had for the Thetas was even stronger now. The few brief conversations she'd had with them had been so superficial that she preferred not talking at all. Elizabeth was sure that in her mother's day they had been wonderful, but now they were stuck-up snobs whose greatest concern was how they looked and how much money everyone had. Joining the Theta Alpha Thetas would be like living with a houseful of Lila Fowlers. Elizabeth smiled to herself. Even Lila's familiar face would almost be a welcome sight here.

She looked around the room and saw the next-best thing: Bruce Patman. Bruce was in a corner, holding court to a bunch of freshmen. He was just as handsome and arrogant as he had been at Sweet Valley High. *I'm not desperate enough to inflict the Patman ego on myself,* Elizabeth decided.

Jessica was dancing with her date and hadn't looked in her sister's direction all evening. And Winston, who was a friendly face, had suddenly disappeared from the staircase.

Elizabeth checked her watch again. *Not much*

*longer,* she told herself. In a little while she'd have to leave to meet Todd, who'd gone to a party with the team. Elizabeth reached for another chip. There was just one question: Was being with the new Todd Wilkins, superjock, going to be any better than being here?

Danny's arms were around her, and her eyes were staring out at the crowded room, but all Jessica could see was the man with the '64 Corvette. She'd wanted to kick herself a thousand times since this afternoon when she realized that although she'd given him her name and address, she hadn't thought to ask him for his.

*It's all right,* Jessica told herself as she swayed to the music. *He'll call; he was flirting with you.* She smiled wryly to herself. *And besides, you dented his car.*

Suddenly the thought of what her sister was going to say when she found out about the accident pushed the dark hair and golden eyes from her mind, and Jessica found herself staring at Elizabeth instead. Only this wasn't her imagination—this was the real Elizabeth, standing at the edge of the room like an uninvited guest.

*Leave it to Liz,* Jessica thought. *This has got to be one of the best parties the world has ever seen, and my sister looks like she's at a lecture on the life cycle of the earthworm.*

Jessica had always known that her twin could be

incredibly boring, but at least in high school she'd always had fun at parties. She'd always talked with everybody and danced a lot. But now that they were in college she'd gotten even more boring. Pretty soon she probably wouldn't bother going out at all. *Not that anybody would notice,* Jessica thought. *For all the effort she's making, she might as well have stayed in her room.*

The music stopped and Danny put a friendly arm around her. By now it was somehow unspoken but clear that their relationship wasn't really going to be romantic. But Jessica felt as though she had made a friend. Not only did he have a good sense of humor and know how to dance, but he loved pineapple pizza. The lovers of pineapple pizza, Jessica had discovered, were few and far between.

"Did I tell you my sister actually prefers the Pi Beta Phis to the Thetas?" she asked as she leaned against him.

Danny smiled. "Come on, Jess. The Pi Betas are okay. Everybody rags them because they're always on some crusade, but most of them are really cool."

"Oh, *please* . . ." Jessica made a face of disbelief combined with nausea. "It's like preferring oatmeal to caviar."

He laughed. "To tell you the truth, *I* prefer oatmeal to caviar. Who wants to eat fish eggs? Yuck."

"Oh, stop it." Jessica gave him a playful shove. "You're just being difficult."

"And you're just feeling guilty for walking out on your sister like that. That's why you jump on everything she does."

Somehow, although she hadn't meant to, she'd found herself telling Danny about moving out of the room with Elizabeth and in with Isabella.

Jessica scowled. It was a good thing Danny was in no danger of becoming her boyfriend. He already knew her too well. "Okay," she admitted, "I do feel a little bit guilty. But you don't know what it's like rooming with someone who drives you crazy. You've got Tom."

Danny looked over to the other side of the room, where his best friend, Tom Watts, was getting ready to leave.

"I know I'm lucky," he said as the music started and he took her into his arms again. "Tom's a great guy."

"I'll bet he says the same about you," Jessica said, but she was already staring dreamily at nothing, thinking about those hazel eyes again.

Jessica was just imagining her first ride in the Corvette, out by the ocean under a moonlit sky, when she realized that the face of the man of her dreams had been displaced by the face of Peter Wilbourne III.

"I believe this is my dance," he was saying, his hand on Danny's shoulder.

To her amazement, Danny started to pull away, but Jessica stopped him. "I believe it's Danny's," she said evenly. And then, remembering Isabella's warning about Peter, she smiled and said, "You can have the next dance if you'd like."

Peter Wilbourne III smiled back. The long white fingers didn't move from Danny's shoulder, and the hard blue eyes focused more intensely on her. "But I don't want to have the next dance," he said softly. "I want this dance."

Jessica suddenly felt cold, as though someone were pouring ice water down her spine. "Well, I'm sorry—" she began.

His look was as cold and sharp as the blade of a knife. "And I'm sorry too," he said, cutting her off. "I can't tell you how disappointed I am in you, sweetheart. When I saw you with Izzy, I thought you looked promising, really promising. 'There's a freshman who can go places,' I said to myself. 'There's a girl who could be a real star.' "

Jessica was trying so hard not to show the nervousness she was feeling and so caught by the intensity of his eyes that she didn't notice Peter edging his way between her and Danny. Not until Danny's hand slipped from her own and she felt Peter Wilbourne's breath on her forehead did she realize what had happened.

He laughed, a sound as pleasant as the rattle of a snake. "It never occurred to me that you would turn me down for scum like this," Peter said, clearly and sharply. He shook his head sadly, raising his voice. "I never dreamed for one second that you were just another piece of white trash. That you were the sort of tramp who would rather dance with our black brother here than with me."

Jessica felt her face go red with fury. "Don't talk to me like that," she hissed, stepping around him to get back to Danny.

"I'll talk to you any way I like," Peter answered. "You're beneath my contempt, sweetheart. I'd sooner take orders from the maid than from a little traitor like you." He laughed again as she moved closer to Danny. "Don't expect *him* to help you," he scoffed. "He's just a cowardly black boy, aren't you, Danny?"

Seeing the sneer on Peter's lips as his eyes fell on Danny, Jessica suddenly remembered what Isabella had told her. Peter didn't hate Danny just because he was black; there was something more there. Peter hated Danny because he was Danny.

Jessica turned to Danny herself, expecting this last insult to finally cause an outburst of anger. After all, Danny was bigger and looked stronger than Peter. But he wouldn't even meet her eyes.

"Leave us alone, Peter," he said in a half whisper. "Nobody wants any trouble—"

"You don't want any trouble, Danny . . ." Peter reached out and pulled Danny's tie, drawing him forward. "I know you don't. You just want to hide behind this white girl here, don't you?" He gave the tie a yank. "Maybe you'd like her to fight your battles for you since you won't do it yourself."

Jessica was suddenly aware that a crowd had gathered around them. She felt so afraid that she couldn't move, couldn't think. Some of the Sigmas started to urge Peter on.

"Get him, Pete," they muttered.

Very low, almost like a hum, Jessica could hear the beginnings of a chant. *Fight fight fight fight* . . .

"Danny," she whispered, reaching out for his hand.

But Danny kept stepping backward, his body rigid, his eyes empty.

"What's the matter, Aunt Jemima?" Peter taunted. "Don't you come with a spine?"

"Don't you come with a brain?"

Jessica spun around as an anxious silence fell over the crowd. A tall, dark-haired boy, lean as a snake but broad and muscular as well, was standing behind Peter. There was nothing empty about the look in Tom Watts's dark eyes; it was furious and cold.

Peter turned slowly around. "This isn't your fight, Watts," he said, sounding distinctly nervous despite his smooth smile.

"It isn't anybody's fight," Tom said. He placed a hand flat against Peter's chest. "Unless you want it to be," he said softly. "And in that case, I'm making it mine."

Peter's smile became even smoother, but his eyes darted nervously at his friends. "Look, Watts," he said, backing off. "I'm not going to bust up a good party for you to play hero for your scared little friend." He turned away. "He isn't worth it." He joined his frat brothers. "Let's party," he ordered.

Jessica moved over to Danny. "Come on," she said. "Let's get out of here."

Tom wanted to get out of there too, but every time he tried, somebody else came up to tell him what a good guy he was. He hated the attention. If it had been anybody but Danny, he probably would have kept right on walking out the door and let what was going to happen, happen.

But he couldn't. He'd gotten halfway across the room, and he knew he couldn't just turn his back. He didn't care about any of these people or the stupid things they did and said, but he cared about Danny. Danny had stood by Tom when his whole world had fallen out from under him, and he never asked any questions or made any demands. He was just there when you needed him. It was only right that Tom should be there when Danny needed him, too.

Tom had just disengaged himself from the embrace of a girl he used to go out with and was pushing his way toward the door when he heard an angry female voice behind him.

"Just a minute," the voice was saying, quietly but forcefully. "I want to tell you something."

Tom and just about everyone near him turned around. He blinked. It was the girl Danny had been with, Jessica something, staring Peter dead in the face. Tom shook his head. This girl looked exactly like Danny's date, but it couldn't be; hadn't he just seen them leave together?

The Sigma president, having recovered himself, smiled smugly and raised one disdainful eyebrow at her. "And who the hell are you?"

The girl didn't hesitate for a second. "It doesn't matter who I am—"

"Well, it matters who I am," he cut in. "Maybe you don't realize it, but I'm Peter Wilbourne the Third."

The girl made a face. "You mean they tried twice before you and they still didn't get it right?"

Some of the onlookers sniggered. Tom let himself smile. This girl was really something. She cared about impressing these people about as much as he did.

Peter Wilbourne III looked as though he was trying to think of some suitable reply to this, but before he could open his mouth the girl went on.

"I'm leaving," she said, "but I wanted to tell you I think you're disgusting. I thought people who went to college were supposed to be at least semi-intelligent. But I was obviously wrong. I'm ashamed to be in the same room with you." She tossed her hair over her shoulder. "You can be sure that it won't happen again."

*No,* Tom told himself. *That definitely isn't the girl Dan was with. This girl isn't like anyone I've ever met before.*

"You better hope it doesn't happen again!"

Peter Wilbourne shouted after her. "For your sake, you really better hope so."

Tom tried to catch the girl's attention as she stormed past him, but she didn't look right or left.

*Watch out, Watts,* Tom warned himself as his eyes followed her through the door. *There goes trouble.*

And he didn't need trouble. He'd had enough trouble for one life already.

Elizabeth was still seething when she arrived at the coffeehouse to meet Todd as they'd arranged. She barely registered the cozy, intimate atmosphere and the candlelit tables. In her mind she was still looking into the Sigma president's smug, smiling face.

"Liz! Liz! Over here!"

Elizabeth stopped at the front of the café and saw Todd waving to her from a corner table. Just the sight of him made her feel better. Everything was all right. There was strong, supportive, sensitive Todd waiting to comfort her, just as he always had. Forgetting the experiences they'd had the past few days, Elizabeth hurried to join him.

"God, you won't believe what happened at the Sigma-Theta rush party," she said as she slid into the chair across from him.

"And wait'll I tell you what happened to me today, Liz," he countered. "I've had the most unbelievable day—"

"The president of the Sigmas called my sister trash and tried to pick a fight with her date," Elizabeth began in a rush.

Todd waved one hand dismissively. "Never mind the Sigmas," he said, obviously not hearing a word she was saying. "The Zetas want me on board, Liz! Isn't that terrific?"

Elizabeth, about to describe the scene between Danny and Peter, could only stare at him.

"The Zetas, Liz. Do you know what that means? The Zetas are *the* fraternity for athletes, and at the dinner tonight the president himself basically told me straight out that they want me on board."

She gave herself a little shake. Todd was justifiably proud and happy. She should put her own distress aside for a few minutes to congratulate him. Elizabeth reached across the table and took his hand. "That's great, Todd," she said sincerely. "It really is. I know how much you—"

"I knew you'd be happy," Todd said as the waitress brought them their menus. "I mean, it's been so great having all the guys on the team be so friendly, but to be a Zeta, too. You should've seen them at the dinner, Liz. These are really good guys . . ."

Elizabeth listened, a smile on her face.

Her smile faded slightly when, having described the Zeta dinner in minute detail, he began to tell her how the other guys on the team had reacted to his good news.

"Bryan said he knew the Zetas would want me

on board," Todd explained, "because Sinclair Ash, the vice president, had told him I was just the sort of guy they were looking for."

By the time their order arrived, she was ready to strangle him. What was all this *on board*? What normal, intelligent person said *on board* every other sentence?

"Can I tell you what happened at the Sigma party now?" she asked, when he finally stopped talking long enough to put a forkful of carrot cake in his mouth.

Todd nodded. "Sure, Liz. I didn't mean to do all the talking." He lifted his coffee cup to his lips, looking at her expectantly.

Elizabeth started telling him about Peter Wilbourne's attack on Danny and Jessica and how Danny had refused to confront him. "And then this amazing guy suddenly appeared from nowhere," Elizabeth continued. "You should've seen him, Todd. He was incredibly well built, you know, and I guess he knew no one was going to try and fight him . . ."

"Is he an athlete?" Todd asked.

The spoonful of triple-chocolate mousse Elizabeth was holding stopped in midair. "What?"

"Is he a jock?"

"I have no idea," she answered, wondering how much of what she was saying was actually going into Todd's head. "I don't even know his name."

Todd shrugged. "I just thought I might know

him," he said. "He sounds like the sort of guy the Zetas would want to have on board too."

Elizabeth leaned against Todd as they walked back to his dorm in the moonlight, their arms around each other. It had taken a while, but eventually the warm atmosphere of the coffeehouse had helped her to relax. Todd had wound down a little himself and stopped getting "on board" everything. At last, it had started to feel as it used to between them.

"I can't believe this is the first time you're seeing my room," Todd said as they took the elevator to the twelfth floor. He leaned over and kissed the top of her head. "I've been waiting to get your opinion on what I should put on the walls," he whispered. "I don't have your sense of style."

Feeling better than she had in days, Elizabeth raised her lips to his. "All you had to do was ask," she whispered back.

Todd laughed nervously as he unlocked the door to his room. "I feel like I should carry you over the threshold or something."

Elizabeth gave him a squeeze. "That's when you get married," she joked. "Not when you move into a jock dorm."

"Yeah, I know that," he said, not turning on the light as they floated into the room. "But this is the first time I've had my own place."

The lights of the campus shone like stars outside Todd's window as Elizabeth melted into his arms. It felt so right, getting lost in his kisses, that she didn't realize things were going farther than they usually did until she felt the urgent way he was trying to pull off her blouse and bra.

"Todd . . ." she whispered as her clothes fell to the floor. The sensation of his hands on her body in the dark room made her skin tingle.

"Elizabeth . . ." His voice was thick and seemed to be coming from more than one direction. He pulled her to the floor.

Part of her knew that things were going too fast and wanted him to stop. But another part—a part that couldn't believe his hands could make her feel like that—didn't. "Todd . . . Todd, please . . ."

"It's all right." His mouth was against her ear. "I don't have a roommate. We're all alone."

She was willing her body to push him off her, but instead it insisted on pushing itself closer. "Todd . . ." With an enormous effort, she managed to pull herself to a sitting position. "Todd, what time is it?" she asked desperately. "I'd really better get back to my dorm."

It took him less than a nanosecond to pull her back down. "You don't have to leave," he said, his voice a purr. "You can stay here tonight."

For a moment she actually thought that he meant that because it was late and he was tired and didn't feel like walking her back to Dickenson Hall, she should crash with him. But as his hands moved down her body she realized the truth. He wanted to make love to her. The part of her that wanted him to stop started shouting louder than the part of her that didn't.

"Todd!" Elizabeth jerked herself away from him so quickly that he landed on the floor with a thud. "We've talked about this. We said we'd wait for the right time."

"But we did wait," he said, pulling her to his chest again. "And this is the right time."

Shaking with something that was anger and something that was more like desire, Elizabeth managed to get to her feet. "It may be the right time for you," she said, practically shouting so she could hear herself against the roar of her heart. "But I don't think it's the right time for me yet."

"But Liz—"

"I mean it." Only by keeping her voice hard and cold could she hide the confusion she was feeling. It would be so easy to fall back in his arms; so easy to stay the night. Too easy. She took a deep breath. "I want to go back to my room now, Todd. Right now."

The light went on so suddenly, she felt as though someone had punched her in the face.

"Sure," Todd said, in a tone she had never heard before. "Whatever you want."

# Chapter Five

The first word that came into Elizabeth's head when she woke up on Saturday morning was: *Enid.*

She opened her eyes. "Alexandra," she corrected herself. "Not Enid, Alexandra."

But it didn't matter. Enid or Alexandra, she was still the best friend Elizabeth had ever had, the person she could talk to about anything, the one who supported her through good times and bad.

Elizabeth rolled over. These were certainly bad times. She wasn't upset about the scene at the Theta-Sigma party. Everything she'd said to that smug creep Peter the Third was true. And it didn't matter if she'd blown her chances with the Thetas, either, because if that was what the Greeks were like, then she didn't want any part of them. She'd come here to get smarter, not more stupid.

But Todd did matter. A heaviness fell over Elizabeth at the thought of him. She'd heard of couples drifting apart once they got to college, but she and Todd were separating at a rate of knots.

She felt lonely and isolated; he'd already found a tight group of friends. She'd gone from being *the* Elizabeth Wakefield, one of the brightest stars of Sweet Valley High, to being a nobody; he was well on his way to becoming *the* Todd Wilkins, the gorgeous basketball star. She wasn't ready to take their relationship any further; Todd definitely was.

Elizabeth climbed out of bed with a sigh. That was what she had to talk to Enid about. There was no one else she could confide in.

The walk back from Todd's dorm last night kept playing itself over in her mind. They hadn't spoken or touched the entire way. Todd had walked beside her, inches that might have been miles between them, his hands in his pockets, as though he hated even the idea that he might brush against her. Seeing them pass by, no one would have thought that they had laughed together, or cried together, or shared so much as a stick of gum.

Elizabeth started going through her dresser, still seeing the expression on Todd's face as he said good night. Cold and remote, it had been the face of someone she didn't know; someone who didn't want to know her. She pulled out a pair of jeans and a black T-shirt to match her mood.

Elizabeth glanced at her watch. If she didn't hurry, she'd be late for breakfast with her best friend.

* * *

Enid threw herself on the still-made bed with a sigh. Was any girl as lucky as she was? Was any girl as happy? "I'm so happy!" she shouted out loud.

She kicked off her shoes and closed her eyes, going over the events of last night for at least the twentieth time. She'd had a blast at the Theta-Sigma party. The Thetas really liked her, and the more she'd known they liked her, the more she had sparkled. It used to be that no one really noticed her at parties because they were too busy looking at Elizabeth, but it wasn't like that anymore. Now she was a star in her own right.

The thought of Elizabeth caused a slight shadow to fall over Enid's happiness. She decided not to think too much about the part where she had lost track of Elizabeth at the party last night. And anyway, although she knew that Elizabeth hadn't seemed to be having a good time, she was still there when Enid and her friends went on to the after-dinner party at Zeta house. Enid had seen her, standing by the food table and looking at her watch.

Enid hugged herself. It was the Zeta party that she wanted to remember in detail. Walking in and seeing Todd over by the window, noticing that he was talking to an absolutely gorgeous sophomore with a stop-traffic smile. Todd looking up and beckoning her over, saying, "This is my friend Alexandra Rollins. We went to high school together." Todd nodding to the dark-haired man with the crooked grin. "Mark Gathers, backbone of the SVU basketball team. Mark, Alex."

"Alex?" he'd said. "That's great. I love girls with boys' names. I think it's so sexy."

Enid opened her eyes, giving herself another hug. *I think it's so sexy.* In four years of high school, no one had ever said the name *Enid* and the word *sexy* in the same breath. Not even by mistake.

Humming happily, she began to undress. She didn't have time to shower before meeting Elizabeth for breakfast, but she was going to have to change. Not only had she been wearing this dress since last night, she'd actually wound up sleeping in it.

Enid caught her reflection in the mirror and gave that pretty, sexy, glowing face a big smile. Who would have thought that after only a week at college, *she* would be spending the night with one of the most popular guys on campus? She, good, old reliable and slightly dull Enid Rollins, shadow of the spectacular Elizabeth Wakefield, had sat up half the night with the most handsome, intelligent, and interesting man she'd ever met.

They'd talked about everything from cereal to politics. She couldn't remember talking so much; certainly not to a guy. And they'd made each other laugh. In fact, they'd talked and laughed so much that when they finally checked the time, it was three in the morning and they didn't feel like coming all the way back across campus to her dorm. "You might as well stay here," Mark had said. "You can have the bed and I'll sleep on the floor." So she had.

Enid pulled on a clean shirt and gave herself another smile. Somehow, sleeping in Mark's bed while he slept on the floor, even though nothing had really *happened*, was the most romantic, grown-up thing she'd ever done.

She ran a brush through her long, wavy hair. She couldn't wait to tell Elizabeth.

*Maybe Todd's right,* Elizabeth told herself as she hurried to breakfast. *Maybe we should sleep together. I mean, it's not like we only just met or something. We love each other. We've been together for years.*

"Hey, look who it is!" someone shouted as she cut across the green. "It's the Martin Luther King fan club."

"Uncle Tom's friend," someone else said.

Not realizing whom they were talking to, Elizabeth glanced over.

Two Sigmas from the night before were leaning against the hood of a metallic blue Toyota, leering in her direction.

"Hey, Little Miss Equal Opportunity," the first one called to her. "Why aren't you out protecting the less fortunate?"

"Somebody should be protecting her," the other one said with a laugh. "After that little scene last night, I think she'll need it."

Elizabeth bit her lip. Was that a threat of some kind? Were these clowns trying to scare her? She turned away quickly. She had too many things on her mind to waste her time worrying about them.

*But I'm really not ready,* Elizabeth argued as she walked through the cafeteria door.

There was no sign of Enid, so she joined the two or three people getting their food. Saturday breakfast was the one meal you could be pretty sure you wouldn't have to stand in line for. Most people preferred sleeping late to eating.

*Just because we're in college now doesn't mean we should immediately jump into bed together. He wasn't asking me to sleep with him two weeks ago. What's the big difference between then and now?*

Faced with the usual wide choice of foods, Elizabeth realized that she wasn't really hungry. She was too hyped up over what had happened last night. She put a grapefruit, a muffin, and a cup of coffee on her tray and went out to find a table.

*Of course I'm right,* Elizabeth assured herself as she stirred milk into her coffee. *Just being in college is no reason to go back on what we decided.*

She looked up to see Enid hurrying toward her. Elizabeth couldn't remember ever seeing her friend look so pretty. It wasn't just her clothes or her make-up, either. In fact, she didn't really look as though she was wearing makeup. No, it was something else. She almost seemed to be glowing from inside.

"Elizabeth!" Enid shrieked. "Wait till I tell you what happened!" She put her tray down and slid into her seat.

Elizabeth was dying to confide in her about Todd, but she put on an interested smile. "What? Tell me!"

Enid shook her head and made a distraught face. "I don't know where to start," she said breathlessly. She giggled. "It's too wonderful, Liz. You just won't believe it! It's so great!"

"Well, go ahead," Elizabeth urged. "Don't keep me in suspense." She made her smile more encouraging.

It wasn't necessary. One minute Enid was sighing and not knowing what to say; the next she was giving Elizabeth a nanosecond-by-nanosecond account of her night with Mark Gathers.

Elizabeth listened in silence, at first with interest, but then with growing concern.

By the time Enid reached the end of her story, she wasn't just glowing, she looked as though she were lit by a klieg light.

"Wait a minute," Elizabeth said. "Are you honestly telling me that you spent the *entire* night with a—a stranger?"

Enid grinned, thinking she was teasing. "He wasn't a stranger, Liz. He was a friend of Todd's." She put down her cup. "And he certainly isn't a stranger now."

Elizabeth stared at her. "You're right," she said, "I don't believe it. I don't believe you spent the night with somebody you don't even know. You must have lost your mind."

Enid held the smile on her face for another instant, and then her mouth went hard. "Oh, come on, Liz. We're in college now. It's not that big a deal."

*We're in college now . . . We're in college now . . . Was that the only thing anyone could say anymore?* "Maybe you don't think it's such a big deal," Elizabeth snapped, half arguing with Enid, half arguing with Todd. "But I do. I thought we came to college to learn and grow, not to jump into bed with the first guy who asks us."

Enid stared at her angrily. "It's not all that easy to learn and grow when your best friend criticizes you every time you try."

There was something as frighteningly final as a gunshot about the way Enid scraped back her chair. "And for your information, Ms. Morality, we didn't sleep together. We hardly kissed. But even if we had, my sex life is none of your business."

Elizabeth watched the girl she used to know so well, the best friend she'd ever have, march out of the cafeteria in a rage.

*Great,* she thought. *My boyfriend's mad at me, my sister's deserted me, and my best friend isn't speaking to me anymore.*

Elizabeth picked up her tray and went back to the food counter. All of a sudden she was starving.

"I wanted to thank you for . . . uh . . . dealing with Wilbourne last night."

Tom looked up. Danny was sitting on his bed,

hunched over as he put on his shoes, his eyes on the floor. Even someone who didn't know Danny as well as Tom did would have been able to tell that though he really was grateful, Danny didn't want to talk about what had happened.

"It's all right," Tom said, returning his attention to ironing his shirt. He didn't want to talk about it either. He wanted to put the whole thing out of his mind and leave it there. "You don't have to thank me. That's what friends are for."

"Well, thanks anyway," Danny muttered. Slowly and meticulously, he began to tie the lace of his running shoe. "I know you figured I—"

"You don't have to explain, man," Tom cut in. "I understand."

Tom understood that the trouble between Peter Wilbourne and Danny went back a long way. Peter had always surrounded himself with sycophants and yes-men, people who did whatever he said, but Danny stood up to him.

Until last winter, that was. Last winter something happened to Danny. It made him stop standing up to Peter. And that was the thing Tom didn't understand. He knew that something had happened at home—something with Danny's older brother—but he didn't know what. And some part of him didn't want to know.

"I don't think I could explain, even if I wanted to," Danny said slowly.

Tom kept his eyes on the iron. "I told you," he

said quickly. "You don't have to explain."

They were best friends, as close as brothers, but they never pried. If Danny wanted him to know something, he'd tell him; if Danny didn't want him to know something, he wouldn't tell him. And vice versa. It was a simple arrangement, and one that worked. There were things, like why Danny had stopped standing up for himself and why Tom had changed so much since they were freshmen, that they never discusssed—and never would discuss. It was enough for Tom to know that Danny wouldn't fight, not even a bastard like Peter Wilbourne. He didn't need to know why.

He turned his shirt and picked up the iron again. Another hiss of steam hid Tom's sigh.

There was one thing about last night that wouldn't stay out of his mind, no matter how hard he tried. Ever since she stormed out of the Theta house, crackling like a fire, the image of the girl with the gold-blond hair and the blue-green eyes kept appearing to him. It followed him back to the dorm, it hung around the lounge while he was trying to watch TV, it kept drifting in and out of his dreams. And here it was now, distracting him while he was trying to get those annoying little creases out of his collar.

Tom looked over at Danny again. *What the hell,* he decided. *There's no harm in just knowing her name.* He gave a little cough. "So, that girl you were with—what's her name, Jessica?—she has a twin sister, doesn't she?"

Danny nodded, getting to his feet. "Elizabeth Wakefield." He grabbed his sweater from the bed. "Did you see her?" he asked, shaking his head. "It's incredible; the two of them look exactly alike, but from what Jessica says, they have about as much in common as a taco and an ice-cream sundae."

Elizabeth. Elizabeth Wakefield.

"No kidding?" Tom started ironing one of the sleeves. "Your girl seemed really nice," he went on, hoping he sounded casual.

"She is really nice." Danny grinned wryly. "Only, she's not my girl. I think we're going to be what's described as 'just good friends.'" He shrugged. "The spark wasn't there. Sometimes it is, and sometimes it ain't."

Tom turned off the iron. "So what's the sister like?" he asked as Danny opened the door.

Danny turned around. "I'm not really sure. According to Jess, she's very serious, a straight-A student, and about as exciting as a cold potato." He winked. "Sounds like she's just your type, Tombo. You want me to ask Jessica to introduce you?"

Tom pulled out the plug. "Oh, right," he said with a laugh. "Do me a favor." But he was still staring at the door after Danny had left.

*Elizabeth,* he was thinking to himself. ***What an ordinary name for such an extraordinary woman.***

"You can't say I didn't warn you about Peter,

because I did," Isabella was saying as she put the coffee cup down on the table. "Though maybe I should have been a little more adamant."

Jessica, only half listening, brought the toast to the table. Although she'd decided that she wasn't going to tell anyone about Mr. Corvette, that didn't mean she was going to stop thinking about him. While she'd been waiting for the bread to pop up, she'd been fantasizing that with his cool good looks and immaculate sense of style, he must be some sort of spy.

Isabella sat down, stretching her long legs. "He's a nasty piece of work. I'm sure the rumors about him being the head of the secret society are true. I bet he's had plastic surgery done so you can't see the 666 tattooed on his forehead."

Jessica set the warm plate on a woven mat. *Of course, he might be a rock musician or a movie star,* she mused, still deep in her fantasy. She frowned. But then she would have recognized him; then she'd probably know his name.

"Jessica!" Isabella was waving a slice of toast in front of her face. "Are you listening to me? This could be really serious. Peter Wilbourne the Third is no one to make an enemy of. Especially when it's obvious that Danny isn't going to protect you. Just think what could have happened if Tom Watts hadn't been there last night. You should've just danced once with Peter when he asked you. You could've saved a lot of trouble."

Jessica spread some jam on her toast. It was hard to get herself all worked up about an egomaniac like Peter the Terrible when her mind was already so occupied. "I don't care about Peter and his prejudices," she said flatly. "And anyway, most of the people at the party were on our side. It was just his pals who were egging him on." She reached for the coffee. "I'm sure the whole thing will blow over by the time classes start."

"Maybe," Isabella said. "But I'd be cool about being seen too much with Danny if I were you. Especially if you're planning on any public clinches."

More like her sister than she might imagine, Jessica raised her head and flicked her hair over her shoulder. "I'll be seen with whoever I want," she said firmly. "But you don't have to worry about any public clinches between me and Danny. It's strictly platonic."

Isabella lifted her cup to her lips. "Well, I'm glad to hear that. You don't want to start your college career on the wrong foot if you can help it. And being beaten up by Peter's henchmen would definitely be the wrong foot." She took a long, slow sip of her coffee, a mischievous look in her beautiful eyes. "Now all we have to do is find the perfect nonplatonic man for you."

"Ummm . . ." Jessica smiled, imagining her own reflection in that pair of golden eyes. "I wonder who he could be."

* * *

"Morning, Winnie!"

"Good morning, Candy!" Winston called. It didn't even bother him that she called him Winnie. Why shouldn't she? The entire British nation had called Winston Churchill Winnie, and he'd won the war.

"Hey, Winnie, dig that robe!"

Winston smiled back. "Morning, Sophie. I like your hair like that." Why should he wind himself up just because she was wearing only cycling shorts and a sports bra? He was a man now, not a boy. Men took that kind of thing in stride.

"Hi, Win! I've fixed your hair dryer for you. You can pick it up whenever you want."

"Thanks, Luce. You can borrow my weights anytime." Luce fixed small appliances, Kate was practically a professional mechanic, and there was a girl on the floor above who did radios and stereos. Living in Oakley Hall was going to save him a fortune in repair bills. He would have been too embarrassed to admit to a bunch of guys that his own mechanical skills were pretty much expended by turning on a light switch, but girls didn't care. They didn't laugh at you and make you feel like a jerk; they just smiled and maybe asked you to do them a favor in return, like pick them up after a late meeting or open a jammed window.

Winston strode into the bathroom, a towel over his shoulder and his toilet kit under his arm. It was

Saturday morning and he was in a wonderful mood.

*I'm in a wonderful mood*, he told himself as he stopped in front of the last sink in the row and put his stuff on the shelf. *Maybe living with girls is like living with cats. Maybe they just take getting used to.*

*That's what it is*, he thought as he eyed himself in the mirror. *I just had to get used to them. Now I'm fine.*

Winston grinned at his reflection. His reflection grinned back. After all, how could he not be fine? The Sigmas loved him. There were a few tricky moments at the party last night when one of the frat guys asked him where he was living, and then when the girls arrived—but those were tiny clouds in an otherwise bright blue sky.

Since the bathroom was empty except for him, Winston risked striking a few poses in the glass as he imagined himself strolling around campus in his Sigma jacket and his RayBans.

Maybe he'd take up skiing or wrestling or even white-water rafting. After all, Sigmas were very athletic guys. Winston hunched in front of the sink, his arms back, his expression stern as he flew down the giant slalom at a speed that had the onlookers breathless, the wind and sun in his face, his body taut and agile. The crowd was going insane. *Go, Winston! Go, Winston!* they chanted. *Go, Winston! Go—*

"Winnie!"

His toothbrush still in his mouth, Winston dove to the floor, pretending to be looking for something that he'd dropped. The door opened and Anoushka slid into the room.

"Winnie! There are a bunch of Sigmas downstairs, asking about you. What do you want us to say? Candy thought you might be a little shy about living here, after the way you snuck out of the party last night as soon as we arrived."

Winston stifled a groan. *Women.* They never missed anything. Why wasn't every cop in the world a woman?

He removed the toothbrush from his mouth. "Anoushka," he whispered, trying to maintain as much dignity as possible, considering that he was on all fours. "Anoushka, I didn't sneak out. I had to—"

"Shhh!" Anoushka yanked the door open and stuck her head out. She slammed it closed again. "It's them!" she announced. "Do you want me to tell them you'll be right out?"

"No!" He scrambled to his feet. "Tell them there's been some mistake. Tell them the Winnie Egbert who lives here isn't me. Tell them it's my twin sister."

Anoushka smiled. "Is there something in this for me?" she asked sweetly.

*How could someone look like such an angel and have such a scheming mind?* Winston wished Anoushka were a boy so he could hit her.

Winston calculated quickly. How much was not being found in the girls' bathroom by the Sigmas worth? Probably about a million.

"What do you want?"

"I want to borrow your car to go shopping later. Benny was going to take me, but you know Benny. He'd rather play football than go shopping, and I hate to take the bus—"

Did she have no mercy? He didn't want to hear about Benny now. "You can have the car!" Winston grabbed her by the shoulders and turned her around. "Just tell them they've got the wrong Egbert and that I live over in Marsden."

Anoushka gave him a shrewd look. "You'll never beat them over there," she said. "Not since you have to wait for them to get out of sight."

He gave her a shove. "I will if you lend me your bike."

Todd stood motionless, the tension easing out of him as the hot water ran down his body. He couldn't get over the way Elizabeth had acted last night.

At first he'd thought she was kidding. After all, it wasn't as though they didn't know each other. It wasn't as though their feelings hadn't been tried and tested over the years.

Todd closed his eyes and raised his face to the spray. He knew they'd never said it in so many words, but he'd thought that once they were living away from home, their relationship would go into the next phase. Why did she think he'd worked so hard to get on the varsity team? Aside from the fact that basketball meant a lot to him, he'd wanted to get a single room so that he and Elizabeth could spend more time together.

But Elizabeth didn't want to spend more time with him. And the time she did spend with him wasn't exactly quality. She'd become so quiet and distant since they'd been on campus that it was hard to believe she was the same girl.

Until last night, he'd thought she was just having some trouble getting used to college life, but now he wasn't so sure. Maybe it had nothing to do with college. Maybe it had to do with him. Everything had been fine when they were in high school. But now that he wanted a real commitment—an adult relationship—she was refusing to give it. All of a sudden nothing he said or did was right. All of a sudden her kisses didn't have enough fire to toast a marshmallow.

Todd turned off the faucet and reached for his towel. Maybe he shouldn't take it so personally. He wasn't the only thing she complained about. She complained about the Greeks, about her sister, about her best friend.

Enid. Todd wrapped the towel around himself and walked out of the shower stall.

This morning, after a fitful night's sleep, he'd gotten up early and gone for a walk. Just as he was returning, he'd seen Enid coming out of the front door of his dorm, looking like she was floating on air.

Elizabeth certainly hadn't been walking on air when he took her home last night. She'd held herself rigid and untouchable, just inches away from him, and hadn't said a word until they reached Dickenson Hall. Then she'd said "Good night." That was it—no kiss, no hug, no "I'll see you tomorrow," no "I'm really sorry, let's talk about it later"—just "Good night."

"A good night was the last thing it was," Todd muttered as he marched into the hall.

Mark was just coming out of his room. He still looked tired, but it was the tired of someone who'd had a wonderful night, not the tired of someone who couldn't sleep because his long-term girlfriend didn't want him to touch her.

Mark's face lit up. "Yo, Wilkins! I've got to thank you for introducing me to Alex. That was the greatest night I've had in a long time."

Todd smiled in the jokey but suggestive way he'd seen the other guys on the team smile when they started talking about girls. "Oh, yeah? And how great was that?"

Mark grinned back. "I'll have you know, Wilkins, that I'm not that kind of guy." He punched him in the arm. "Anyway, I'd never make a move on a girl like Alex. I like her too much. I'd be afraid she wouldn't respect me in the morning."

"Oh, yeah?" Todd gave him a knowing look. "Then who was it I saw coming out of here this morning? Alex's double?"

Mark raised an eyebrow. "Boy, you were up early. Were you walking Elizabeth back home?"

Rather than answer, Todd just kept smiling and looking knowing. If Mark thought he was sleeping with Elizabeth, that was all right with him.

"It's okay for you guys who've been going out with the same girl for half your life," Mark said. "But we jocks who have always played the field have to go slow in this relationship game." He punched him again. "Anyway, I'd better get going or I'll be late. But thanks again, Todd. You may just have changed my life."

Todd went back to his room, wondering if his life was changing too. If guys like Mark were slowing down, maybe guys like him should start speeding up. Mark might have been joking, but he was right. There were an awful lot of women on this campus who liked jocks.

Todd pulled on his jeans and a T-shirt and gave himself a once-over in the mirror. He looked good. That wasn't vanity, that was the truth.

He brushed back his hair. And some of those women were older women, women with experience. Women who weren't afraid of a little more experience, either.

# Chapter Six

As Jessica left History 101.8 on Monday morning and headed to her second class, she couldn't help thinking that having to take classes was a major bore—the big cloud in the silver lining of college life. She didn't want to be stuck in a room listening to someone drone on about people who were dead and things that had happened hundreds of years ago. She wanted to be out experiencing life and buying clothes to wear to that experience.

Jessica checked her schedule again. At eleven she was supposed to be in room 25 in Denton Hall for introductory philosophy with Professor Malika.

*Who wants to be introduced to philosophy?* Jessica wondered glumly as she climbed the stairs of Denton. *I'd much rather be introduced to Mr. Corvette.*

Jessica entered room 25 with a martyred sigh. She hadn't even meant to sign up for philosophy, but the adviser at the philosophy department desk had been so cute that before she realized what had happened he was handing her back her computer card and telling her he hoped she enjoyed the class.

Jessica headed for a seat in the middle of the large, crowded classroom. Experience had taught her that if you sat in the front, teachers would notice when you weren't paying attention, but that if you sat at the back, they expected you not to be paying attention and would always ask you questions to make sure you were still awake. If you sat in the center, they hardly knew you were there.

Professor Malika shut the door and walked to the front of the room. He was not the cute adviser at the philosophy registration table. He was a balding, middle-aged man with glasses and a slight stoop. Settling as comfortably into her chair as possible, she opened her notebook, faced the front of the room, and began to think about young men who drove expensive cars.

She couldn't understand it. Here it was, the first day of classes, and she still hadn't heard from him. Why had he taken her name and number if he didn't intend to call? Every time she replayed their conversation after the crash, she became more and more convinced that he'd been flirting with her. What about that glint in his eyes? What about that smile? Sure, he'd pretended to be angry and upset, but he wasn't really. She'd seen enough men angry in her life to know the difference—especially when she was the one who had made them angry.

And besides, he hadn't even contacted the insurance company yet. Her mother had made both her and Elizabeth promise to call every Sunday, and though Jessica had dreaded making the phone call last night because of the lecture she was sure her father would give her about automotive safety, Mr. Wakefield hadn't said a word.

Jessica shifted in her chair. Sunlight was falling across the trunk of the Corvette, and in its deep shine she could see the reflection of a tall, dark man with an enigmatic smile. Who was he? Why hadn't he called?

The boy next to Jessica nudged her arm. Jessica looked around in annoyance, about to give him a piece of her mind, when she realized he was gesturing toward the front of the room. Professor Malika must have been trying to get her attention. She turned with one of her sweetest smiles.

Professor Malika smiled back. "Thank you, Miss, ah—"

"Wakefield." She sat up a little straighter, wishing she knew what was going on. "Jessica Wakefield."

"Wakefield," he repeated. "Now, if you'd be good enough to answer my question . . ."

*I'd love to answer your question,* Jessica thought. *If only I knew what it was.*

"Of course," she said. She gave him one of her three-hundred-watt smiles and looked at him expectantly. It was a technique that used to work in high school.

There was half a second of silence while she smiled at the philosophy professor and he stared back at her like a rabbit in the headlights of an oncoming car. And then he said, "What is the purpose of philosophy?"

The phantom image of Mr. Corvette shimmered in front of Professor Malika. Jessica's smile went up to six hundred watts. Maybe the cloud in the middle of her silver lining wasn't as large or as dark as she'd feared. "To discover the truth," she said confidently.

"Truth!" cried Professor Malika, looking surprised but pleased. "Truth is the purpose of philosophy. Very good, Miss Wakefield. I'm glad someone has a basic understanding of the subject."

Jessica fell back into her daydreams. College was going to be even easier than she'd dared hope.

Tom stopped in the doorway of his film class, checking out the room. The film majors, looking intense and superior, were gathered at the front. The kids who were taking the course because it was the only thing they could fit in their schedule were bunched up in the middle. And at the back were a couple of big-league jocks with the usual cluster of admiring girls around them, listening to them discuss bombs and squib kicks as though they were the most fascinating things in the world.

Tom stepped into the room and walked over to a second-row seat at the side. In the old days, if he'd decided to take a course on Hollywood comedies of the '30s and '40s it would have been because he figured he could skate through it without too much trouble. Anybody could watch a movie, right? And in the old days he'd be sitting at the back with the campus heroes, feeling like a big man because he knew how to throw a ball.

He read through the assigned text while he waited for the instructor to arrive. These were not the old days. Now he was taking film because he was interested; he was interested in everything. Life was too short not to get all you could out of it.

And he sat at the front with the film freaks because they still thought of him as Wildman Watts, superjock, and left him alone. In the old days, all Tom wanted was a good time and to be surrounded by people who told him how great he was. Now he'd rather be on his own than have a bunch of insincere good-time friends. Life was too short to waste.

The two people sitting beside him started arguing about who was better, Frank Capra or Howard Hawks.

Tom closed his book and looked out the window. *Who cares who's better?* he asked silently. *They're both dead now. Being better won't do either of them any good.*

He watched the students hurrying to their classes and thought about crowd scenes. You saw these people all the time, but you never knew them; they just walked back and forth in your life. *And for all I care they can keep walking,* Tom thought as a flash of golden yellow caught his eye. He turned. It was Jessica Wakefield, striding down the path by herself.

He missed a breath. It wasn't Jessica; it was her sister, Elizabeth. Identical as they were, he was sure it wasn't Jessica. Jessica moved like someone who was sure of everything, just as he used to. But Elizabeth moved like someone who'd learned that you couldn't be sure. Tom leaned forward, watching Elizabeth disappear into the English building.

Something about Elizabeth Wakefield made him wonder if he really wanted *everyone* to walk by.

Jessica was the first one on her feet when the class finally ended. She wasn't going to have any problem getting a good grade out of Professor Malika as long as she kept smiling.

She glanced at the clock tower as she fled the philosophy hall. If she hurried, she could dump her books in her room before she met Denise for lunch.

"It's just me!" Jessica called as she pushed open the door of the suite. She hadn't expected Isabella to be home, but the door was unlocked.

"I thought you said you'd be out all—" she began, but the words shriveled up in her throat. There was someone stretched out on the couch, reading a magazine, and it wasn't Isabella Ricci.

Slowly, as though he'd only just realized someone had come into the room, he turned toward her.

"I was hoping you'd come back before lunch."

How could anyone have such an insolent and yet such a charming smile? Today he was dressed in jeans and a faded flannel shirt, with dirty old black high-tops on his feet. Jessica stood silent for a few seconds, trying to get her heart back to its normal beat.

He dropped the magazine and sat up. "You're not a very good hostess, are you?" he asked. "You haven't even offered me a cup of coffee. If you're not nicer to me, I might not come back."

*Play it cool,* Jessica told herself. *Don't let him rattle you. Play it cool.*

She forced her legs to carry her to the table and threw down her books. "I don't remember inviting you in the first place," she said, keeping her face impassive. "Just how did you get in here?"

"These locks aren't exactly high security, you know." Insolent smile; face of an angel. "And anyway, you did invite me when you rammed into my car." He got to his feet, his hands in his pockets. "You didn't think I'd forgotten, did you? You didn't think I got home and the Corvette had miraculously healed itself?"

She wasn't going to let him intimidate her just because she found it so hard to look at him and think at the same time. Jessica raised her chin. "I thought you were going to contact the insurance company. I told you they'd take care of it."

He came toward her, stopping only a few feet away. "I changed my mind about that." A smile as sweet and slow as molasses appeared on his face. "It's not insurance money that I want."

She felt as though the air had suddenly been drained from the room. There were flowers on the table and traces of her and Isabella's perfume in the air, but all she could smell was him.

"What do you want?" she asked, surprised to discover she could still speak.

"Don't worry," he said, brushing a strand of hair away from her cheek. His touch was as gentle as a butterfly. "I'll let you know when I'm ready."

He was gone before she'd quite absorbed the fact that he was there. As she picked his magazine off the floor to stick it in the rack with Isabella's, a plain black card fell out. Across it he'd written his name in silver ink. *Michael McAllery.*

"Michael McAllery," Jessica read out loud. "Well, how do you do?"

Enid made her way through the lunch line, talking to Elizabeth in her head. *If you can't accept me as I am, then maybe you're not the friend you thought you were,* she was saying. *I'm not going to stay in your shadow just to make you feel better.*

She dropped a sandwich and an apple onto her tray.

*If you can't see me as anything but good old Enid, maybe I should stick to people who never knew me then,* she continued.

She smacked down a bag of potato chips and a

Diet Coke. *I'm sorry, Elizabeth,* she said as she banged her tray down next to the register, *but I think you and I have come to a parting of the ways. You want to stay just where you are, and I want to move on.*

Ever since their argument on Saturday morning, Enid hadn't been able to think about much else. The trouble was that although she was no longer speaking to Elizabeth Wakefield in the flesh, she couldn't stop arguing with her in her head. Emerging into the dining room, she turned left and walked purposefully to the window table where Shaun, Jan, and Delia were sitting. They were still talking about Friday night.

"I really, really hope I get pledged to Theta," Delia was saying as Enid took the seat beside her. "They are just the coolest."

Shaun giggled. "Plus the fact that they're paired with Sigma doesn't hurt. Those guys are gorgeous."

"I still think it's too bad about your friend Elizabeth," Jan said. "I hear that Peter Wilbourne's going around bad-mouthing her."

"I'm sure it's just a bunch of lies," Shaun said.

Jan shrugged. "Maybe. But nobody makes Peter look like a fool without paying for it. I've heard that when he doesn't like someone, things just have a way of going wrong for them."

Enid was busy unwrapping her sandwich and didn't look up. She had already left the party by the time Elizabeth caused the scene everybody was talking about. She hadn't heard about it until Saturday. Even as angry as Enid was with Elizabeth, she had to admire her for standing up to Peter like that. She knew Elizabeth had been right—even if she secretly thought she'd been pretty foolish to throw her college social life away like that. After all, Danny Wyatt was built like a tank; he didn't need Elizabeth to defend him.

Delia shook her head. "I wouldn't want to be her for anything," she said. "Jan's right. From what I hear, Peter Wilbourne can be brutal."

"And from what I hear, he's not the only one," Jan said.

The others all looked at her quizzically.

"What are you talking about?" Shaun asked.

Jan lifted a forkful of rice salad into the air. "I overheard some girls in my art class talking about this psychic in town who's predicting some brutal murderer will strike here on Halloween night."

"Oh, come on!" Enid cried, happy to get the conversation away from her ex–best friend. "What are you talking about, 'Nightmare at Sweet Valley U'?"

"Hey, it's not *my* prediction," Jan said. "I'm just telling you what I heard. These girls said this psychic really knows his stuff. They say he predicted the earthquake in San Francisco, and that hurricane in Florida."

Shaun smirked. "Oh, yeah. And he probably predicted the assassination of Lincoln, too."

Enid laughed. "I agree with Shaun. The thing with these psychics is that they always tell you when they got something right, but they never tell you all the thousands of times they were wrong."

Delia put down her glass. "I don't believe in any of that stuff," she said. "As far as I'm concerned, if you can't eat it, wear it, or put it on the wall, it doesn't exist."

Jan pointed her fork at Delia. "There's more in heaven and earth, Delia Thomas, than is dreamt of in your philosophy."

"Oh, ha ha ha." Delia put on a haughty face. "I know you're quoting Shakespeare, Jan. I *am* in college now."

*That's right,* Enid thought. *We are in college now.* And the phrase suddenly sent Enid's mind back to the same subject it had been with all day: Elizabeth Wakefield.

Elizabeth had arrived at lunch in a buoyant mood. She couldn't wait to see Todd, to tell him how much better she was feeling. Not only was she looking forward to the arrival of her new roommate, but she was feeling excited now that classes had begun. Even though she hadn't gotten all the courses she'd wanted, she really liked the teachers. Just settling down to schoolwork again cheered her up. She sighed to herself. Unlike people, with schoolwork you knew where you stood.

But after having waited for twenty minutes, Elizabeth's mood was beginning to sour. She swallowed the last spoonful of pudding and put down the spoon. She hated eating alone, but the other option had been to sit here by herself with a full tray, staring expectantly at the door while she waited. At least eating had given her something to do.

Elizabeth glanced toward the entrance. *Why don't you just face the truth?* she asked herself. *He's not coming. He's got something better to do.* Her eyes fell on a crowded table across the room. Sitting in the middle, smiling radiantly and looking even prettier than she had in high school, was Enid. *Alexandra,* Elizabeth corrected herself.

She started stacking her dishes. Todd had been busy all weekend with the team, but they had managed to have a cup of coffee together last night. The atmosphere between them had been stiff and awkward, but not unfriendly. And it *was* Todd who suggested having lunch today.

*Maybe he had to make a change in his schedule or something,* Elizabeth told herself. *I'll give him ten more minutes. I'll go get another dessert, and if he's not here by the time I'm done, then I'll leave.*

In the end, she gave him fifteen minutes and twenty-three seconds, then picked up her books and left the cafeteria. She avoided passing Enid and her friends, but she couldn't help feeling that everyone was watching her. Watching and wondering what was wrong with her, because she had no friends.

* * *

By the time she reached her dorm, Elizabeth wanted to get inside her room, lock the door, and never come out. Not only had she just experienced one of the most depressing lunches of her life, but as she was coming across the campus she'd run into two Sigmas who'd given her a hard time about Friday night. They'd blocked her path and refused to let her pass. Even though it was broad daylight and they'd pretended they were just fooling around, Elizabeth had sensed a menace in their smiles.

*All I seem to do around here is make enemies and lose friends,* she told herself unhappily as she hurried down her hall.

She stopped in front of room 28, fumbling in her pocket for her key. But before she could put it in the lock, the door swung open suddenly.

Elizabeth blinked in surprise. Standing in front of her was a strikingly beautiful girl with masses of honey-blond curls and the reddest lips and most heavily made-up eyes Elizabeth had ever seen on anyone who wasn't acting in a play. Behind her, boxes and furniture were piled so high that the beds had disappeared.

"Hi," the girl drawled in a soft southern accent. "I'm Celine Boudreaux, your new roommate."

The door shut behind Elizabeth with a thud. Celine looked up from the drawer she was filling with silky underwear and lacy bras. Her pretty mouth curled unattractively and her eyes narrowed.

"I'd appreciate it if you didn't smoke in our room," she mimicked in a babyish voice. "I hope you don't mind, but I like to keep things neat."

She got up and took a cigarette from the pack on her dresser, lighting it with her brushed-gold lighter.

"My God," Celine said in her own voice. "I can't believe I've escaped Granny Boudreaux and the Simeon Academy for Girls, only to wind up living with Little Miss America."

She opened her roommate's closet, scattering ashes as she began looking through Elizabeth's clothes. "At least she won't have to worry about me borrowing her things," Celine muttered.

She pulled out several skirts and blouses and a pink cotton dress. "Lord help us," she cried, her mouth pinched in distaste. "I didn't think they made things like this for girls over twelve."

She went over to Elizabeth's dresser. "Now, what have we here?" she asked, taking up the photograph of Elizabeth and Todd with their arms around each other. "What's a sweetheart like you doing with a boring princess like this?" she asked the image of Todd. "I'd dump her if I were you. Start having some fun."

After rummaging through the things on top of the dresser, she started going through the drawers themselves.

"This girl doesn't even have a secret life," Celine drawled as she lifted slacks and shirts, looking for love letters and some form of birth control.

She held a pajama top up between two fingers. "Bless my granny's gout," Celine said. "I'll bet the princess is a virgin."

Celine lit another cigarette, closing her eyes while she inhaled deeply.

The one thing she wanted right now was to leave the past behind. Celine's pale blue eyes opened again as a shudder ran through her slender body. No, she wanted more than that. She wanted to set it on fire and scatter its ashes over the ocean.

That was why she had chosen Sweet Valley U. She couldn't have gotten farther from Louisiana and its nightmare memories than here. And after all those years with Granny Boudreaux breathing down her neck and all those horrible boarding schools with their regulations and stuck-up prisses, she had also been hoping to find someone like herself here. Someone with life, spirit, and a sense of fun. Someone who didn't live by the rules.

And instead she'd been given a person for whom the rules were made in the first place. Someone who didn't take any risks, who did what she'd been told.

Celine looked at Elizabeth's desk. Elizabeth's notebooks were neatly stacked on one side, her textbooks on the other, and her pens and sharpened pencils were neatly collected in a glass jar. There was no dust, no piles of papers, no stray stockings or trails of ash. It didn't look like a real desk to Celine; it looked like a desk in a magazine ad. Just as Elizabeth was like a girl in a magazine, perfect and bloodless.

She blew a smoke ring across the room. "Well, we'll just have to shake you up a little, honey," she said, her voice sweeter than syrup.

*It's impossible*, Elizabeth was telling herself as she marched across the quad. *You can't totally loathe someone after only fifteen minutes.* She pictured Celine's face with its pouty red mouth and its long, fluttering eyelashes. She recalled the heavy, flowery smell of her perfume. She heard her soft, sticky-sweet voice. "I know there are rules in the dorm, sugar, but rules are there to be broken, aren't they?" Elizabeth shuddered. "I hope you don't mind," Celine's voice went on, "but I'm going to need a little more closet space."

Elizabeth stopped in the middle of the quad, wondering what to do next. She had nearly two hours to kill before her next class. "You know what, sugar?" Celine's voice was still going in her head. "If you could just move your dresser against your bed, then when the rest of my things finally get here, I'll have a place for my granny's chair."

*Snack bar*, Elizabeth decided suddenly. Even though she'd just had lunch, she was going to need a cup of coffee and maybe a brownie to calm her down enough to be able to study.

As soon as she stepped through the door, Elizabeth began to feel better. The snack-bar smells of coffee, fries, and burgers put the smells of powder, perfume, and menthol cigarettes out of her mind.

*Maybe Celine isn't as bad as she seems,* she told herself as she got in line. *You really shouldn't judge people by first impressions. And she is friendly.* Elizabeth put a peanut-butter brownie on her tray.

Friendly was an understatement. Celine had only been in Dickenson for a couple of hours and already she knew half the girls on the floor. Elizabeth felt her blood pressure rising again. She took a chocolate-chip cookie, too. Not only did Celine know half the girls on the floor, but she had loaned one of them Elizabeth's camera and another the pen Elizabeth's grandparents had given her for graduation.

Elizabeth paid for her food and found a table in a corner by the window. *Maybe you're being a little petty,* she scolded herself. *After all, Celine had no way of knowing how expensive that pen is. And you'd more or less already told Lilli that she could use your camera.* Elizabeth bit intothe brownie, her irritation over Celine fading away. *Once you get to know her a little better, everything will be fine.*

Winston entered the cafeteria warily, standing in

the doorway for a few seconds, just looking around. Most of the Sigmas lived and ate in the frat house, but once in a while one turned up in the cafeteria. He saw a few of his dormmates, but no blue jackets. He took a deep breath and strode in.

Winston grabbed a tray with a sigh. *I'm only eighteen. I shouldn't have to live under all this stress.*

On Saturday morning he'd managed to beat the Sigmas to Marsden by avoiding roads and riding Anoushka's bike across the lawn. He was a little breathless as he strolled out of the hall and into the frat guys, but they didn't seem to notice. They'd been looking all over for him, they said. One of the brothers had a printout of the freshman housing list, but the only W. Egbert they'd found lived in Oakley. They'd laughed heartily about that. "You must think we're a bunch of idiots, looking for you in a girls' dorm," Bill Montana, the sky diver, had said. Winston had laughed the loudest. They'd all gone to breakfast then, and the Sigmas had invited him to a rush dinner that night. By the time he got back to his room, he'd been feeling pretty pleased with himself. *Clever Winnie,* he'd told himself as he drifted off to sleep. *You're made.*

Sunday he'd woken up in a cold sweat. All of a sudden he realized that he wasn't quite as clever as he thought. What if the Sigmas *called* Marsden? What if a couple of his new buddies decided just to drop by? Winston had felt his heart crawl down to his toes. His name wasn't even on the dorm directory. No one there had ever heard of him. *I'm dead,* he thought. *I might as well go buy myself a coffin and get inside.*

It was Maia who came to the rescue. She remembered that Betsy Spuma on the second floor went out with a guy who lived in Marsden. For the loan of the Beetle for the next four Fridays, Betsy's boyfriend was willing to write Winston's name on the room list and field all calls. But that, of course, hadn't been the end of his problems.

Winston decided to go for the hot meal. He needed his strength.

First thing this morning, there'd been a call from Betsy's boyfriend saying that Bill had left a message that he and some of the other guys would pick him up to go to breakfast. Winston barely had time to brush his teeth so that he could be waiting outside Marsden when the Sigmas arrived.

"Do you think I could have just a little more of the chicken?" Winston asked the server. He was sure he'd read somewhere that protein was good for stress.

"Don't tell me," the girl behind the counter said, "you're a growing boy."

*Growing old,* Winston thought as she handed him his plate.

# Chapter Seven

Elizabeth came out of the bathroom, a towel wrapped around her just-washed hair, and her shower things in her arms. At the door to her room she stopped to listen. *Please let her be asleep,* she silently prayed. Elizabeth's heart hit the floor as the sound of a relentless drumbeat drifted through the door. Celine was the only person Elizabeth had ever known who liked to wake up to incredibly loud heavy-metal music. But then, Celine was the only person Elizabeth had ever known who lived on coffee and cigarettes, kept a fifth of bourbon in her hair-dryer case, and couldn't discuss the weather without managing to bring up sex.

In fact, three weeks of sharing a room with Celine had convinced Elizabeth that Celine was like no other human she had ever encountered. She was so arrogant and self-centered that she made Lila Fowler, seem humble by comparison.

Elizabeth closed her eyes and counted to ten. *Please be dressed,* she begged. *Please be dressed and on your way out of here.*

Taking a deep breath, she opened the door. Celine was sitting on Elizabeth's bed, smoking a cigarette and polishing her nails.

"Um, Celine," she said as calmly as she could manage. "It's eight in the morning. Do you think you could turn that down?"

Celine didn't look up.

Elizabeth went straight to Celine's expensive sound system and turned it off.

That got her attention. "What'd you do that for?" she demanded.

"It's eight A.M., Celine," Elizabeth repeated. "I'm sure everybody on the hall would appreciate a little peace and quiet."

Celine gave her a dismissive look. "You know what my granny always says. You'll get all the peace and quiet you want when you're dead."

Elizabeth ground her teeth together. She was almost as sick of Celine's granny as she was of Celine. No matter what Elizabeth suggested—that Celine hang up her clothes, that she not smoke in the room, that she stop using Elizabeth's shampoo and borrowing her towels because she was too lazy to do a load of laundry—Celine had some stupid saying from her granny as an answer.

"Could you do that on your own bed?" Elizabeth asked as she started to put her things away.

Celine blew on her nails. "No can do, sugar."

"No can do?" Elizabeth stopped searching for the hair dryer Celine always borrowed. "What do you mean, 'No can do'?"

Celine turned to her with one of her more radiant smiles. "That bedspread cost a fortune," she answered sweetly. "My granny would just kill me if I got any polish on it."

"And I'll kill you if you get any on mine," Elizabeth said, mimicking Celine's syrupy voice.

"Oh, don't go gettin' your underpants all in a twist." Celine got up, scattering cotton balls over the floor. "I'm all done, sugar. And anyway, I have to hurry; I'm meeting the most gorgeous guy for breakfast. I swear his backside looks better than the one on the lead singer of Lethal Substance."

"I'm so happy for him," Elizabeth mumbled.

But Celine was already out of the room, the door banging shut behind her.

Elizabeth grabbed one of Celine's shoes that was under her desk and threw it after her. Giving up on the hair dryer, she went over to her bed and stared down at the open box of cookies, the used cotton balls and emery boards, and the full ashtray Celine had left there. "Death's too good for her," Elizabeth said in a voice close to breaking. "It would have to be slow torture."

Not only had Celine been doing her nails and smoking on Elizabeth's bed, she'd been eating Elizabeth's food as well. Furious, she started dumping everything in Celine's wastebasket—the only space Celine never filled.

When she was through brushing the crumbs onto the floor, she collapsed on the bed herself. Not for the first time, Elizabeth wished that she hadn't let Jessica talk her out of bringing her stuffed animals with her. She could really use something soft and blue to hug this morning.

"I don't know how much more of this I can take," she said as she reached into the wastebasket and took out the box of cookies.

Celine leaned across the table, her beautiful mouth in a pout, her blue eyes troubled. "You have no idea what I have to put up with. I'm just not used to being treated this way."

The boy, whose name was either Jeff or Joe, she wasn't quite sure which, nodded sympathetically. "Roommates can be a real drag," he agreed. "Yours really sounds awful."

Celine arched one perfect eyebrow, shuddering delicately. "Awful? All she does is moan and nag all the time. It's like rooming with somebody's mother." She put on her Elizabeth Wakefield voice, which was not sweet and hushed like her own but loud and slightly whiny. "Don't do that, Celine. Don't do this, Celine," she mimicked. "Celine, where's my shampoo? Celine, did you leave the light on? Celine, don't forget to lock the door. What time are you coming back tonight, Celine?" Her foot accidentally brushed against his ankle. "That's why I'm having so much trouble in physics," she said forlornly. "I can't even work in our room, she makes me so unhappy."

Jeff or Joe, or perhaps it was Jason, smiled. "Don't worry about that. I'll give you all the help you need. I've always been good in science."

Celine looked deep into his eyes. "You're so sweet," she purred. "I don't know what I'd do if it weren't for you."

He stared back, looking like a man about to drown. The sudden alarm on his watch made him jump. "Wow. I'd better get going or I'll be late for math." He gathered up his books. "So, I'll meet you after dinner to do the homework, right?"

Celine was in the middle of nodding when a look of devastation came onto her face. "Oh, no," she gasped. "I can't tonight! I'm so far behind in everything because of *her* that I have to try to catch up in history tonight." She sighed so heavily that the gold C around her neck heaved up and down. "Oh, what am I going to do? I'll never get my physics homework done in time."

Jeff, Joe, or Jason got to his feet. "I'll tell you what," he said. "Why don't I meet you in the morning and you can copy mine this one time? Then tomorrow night or the night after we can work together and I'll show you what to do."

"Why, what a brilliant idea. I do believe you're

a genius." She grabbed his hand. "And an angel. An absolute angel."

Jeff, Joe, or Jason blushed. "Well . . ." he said. "Well . . . I . . . Maybe you . . ."

Celine gave him a gentle shove. "You'd better go," she said. "I'd hate to think I made you late for math." She smiled. "I'll see you outside the library at ten, how's that?"

"That's great," he said, bumping into someone coming along the aisle as he backed away. "Thanks, Celine. I'll see you then."

Celine leaned back in the booth, watching him dash out of the snack bar. *Well, that takes care of physics,* she thought happily. Some skinny boy with acne and glasses was doing her history, and a fat sophomore with bad breath was doing her English. Now that her work was taken care of, Celine looked around the room for someone she knew.

She was just about to go back to the dorm and take a nap when a tall, handsome boy stepped through the door. A tall, handsome boy she recognized but didn't know. *You'll do,* Celine said to herself. *You'll do just fine.*

The aroma of hamburgers and french fries assaulted Todd as soon as he opened the snack-bar door. He hadn't realized how hungry he was. He and Mark had had a few free hours and decided to play some ball, but they'd gotten so engrossed in their game that they played through lunch.

Todd joined the line. Lately he was so completely caught up in basketball and the team that he was always forgetting everything else. Especially Elizabeth. A pang of guilt even stronger than his pang of hunger hit him. Out of the maybe twenty times in the last two or three weeks that he and Elizabeth had arranged to meet, he must have forgotten at least half of them.

He ordered a double cheeseburger and a double order of fries and leaned against a poster for the Halloween dance taped to the wall. Of the ten plans with Elizabeth he hadn't forgotten, at least five had had to be canceled because of something that came up with the team.

Elizabeth blamed him, of course. Everything was his fault. He wasn't making enough of an effort. But how much of an effort did she expect him to make when all she did when they were together was complain or sulk? Or ice him. She was always accusing him of not loving her anymore, but when he said that he did love her, that he loved her so much he wanted more than anything to spend the night with her, she froze up completely.

*I'm in a no-win situation,* Todd told himself as he watched the guy at the grill flipping burgers. *And I'm beginning not to care.* If there was one thing he was learning at college, it was that there were a lot of pretty girls around. Girls who were cool and smart and a lot of fun, the way Elizabeth used to be. Girls who weren't afraid of getting close, the way Elizabeth was.

Something incredibly light and warm touched his arm. "A penny for your thoughts, Todd Wilkins," said a female voice as gentle as a caress. "A brand-new, bright shiny penny."

Todd turned to find himself staring into the face of one of the most beautiful girls he'd ever seen. Her perfume had not only obliterated the smell of the hamburgers, it made him want to bury his face in her hair. "Excuse me?" he said. "Do I know you?" He was sure he didn't. She wasn't the kind of girl you forgot.

"No, you don't. But I know you. I look at your picture every day." She laughed. "I guess you could say I've been admiring you from afar."

Todd shook his head. "I don't think I—"

She laughed again, extending her hand. "I'm Celine Boudreaux. I share a room with Elizabeth." Her grip was firm and lingering. "She talks about you all the time."

"Double cheese and fries!" the guy at the grill shouted, banging a plate down on the counter.

"Oh, right." Todd hoped he was hiding his shock. From the description of Celine he'd had from Elizabeth, he'd expected her to look like the Wicked Witch of the West. "Celine. Of course. Elizabeth talks about you, too."

"Oh, isn't she sweet . . ." Celine smiled. "I just love rooming with Elizabeth. I come from Louisiana, as you may have guessed, and I don't know anyone here. I don't know what I'd do without her. It's not always easy to make new friends, is it?"

Todd picked up his lunch, feeling even more annoyed with Elizabeth than he had before. *This poor girl,* he was thinking. She was grateful to Elizabeth, and all Elizabeth ever did was complain about her.

"I know," Todd said. "It can be tough adjusting to college. Especially when you come from another state and everything. You must be lonely."

"I'd be devastatingly lonely if it weren't for your girlfriend," she answered. "It would be just too awful to bear."

Todd was sure he'd never seen a blue the color of her eyes before. "Are you sitting with anyone?" he asked as he moved down the line.

Celine shook her head sadly. "No, no. I'm on my own."

"Well, what do you know?" Todd said. "So am I."

Celine brushed against him as she poured herself a soft drink. "I can't tell you how happy I am that I bumped into you."

Todd smiled. He was feeling pretty happy about it himself.

"Yuck," Jessica said, pretending to shudder. "This is revolting." She pushed her history textbook away from her. "I don't know why they think showing you pictures of dead bodies is going to help you remember what happened back then."

"You'd better get used to looking at dead bodies," said Isabella. She pointed to the photograph in Jessica's book with her pen. "Because according to Barnabas Montoya, that's exactly what this campus is going to look like on Halloween."

Jessica groaned. "Oh, not you, too. What is it with everyone in this school? How can you believe a silly rumor like that?"

"How do you know it's a silly rumor?" Isabella leaned forward, her eyes bright with excitement. "How do you know it isn't true that on Halloween night a blood-crazed psychopath is going to go on a killing rampage in a college building shaped like an X?"

Jessica put on a gullible face. "Oh, gee," she said. "I wonder which building that could be?" She widened her eyes. "It couldn't be Xavier Hall, could it? Where the big dance is being held?"

Isabella flicked a paper clip at her. "You can scoff, Ms. Wakefield, but remember, he who laughs last laughs best. And this time he who laughs last may be holding a very sharp ax."

Jessica laughed and got up. "How about a cup of coffee? I'm exhausted from studying."

"Jessica . . ." Isabella gave her a mocking smile. "We've been sitting here for only an hour, and most of the time we've been talking."

Jessica looked over her shoulder. "Does that mean you don't want coffee?"

Isabella laughed. "No, I want coffee." She leaned back in her chair. "So what's this new interest of yours in vintage cars?" she asked. "Your sister's not going to be too pleased if you turn in the Jeep for a Thunderbird, you know."

Jessica poured water into the espresso machine. "What are you talking about? I'm not into vintage cars."

"Then whose magazine was that I found in with my fashion magazines?" Isabella asked, following her into the kitchenette.

Jessica was glad that she had her head bent so that Isabella couldn't see she was blushing. As close as she and Isabella had become over the last few weeks, she still hadn't mentioned Michael McAllery to her. If it had been any other guy, Jessica would have told Isabella everything right away. But Michael was too important. He wasn't just another guy to be dated and cast aside when the next one came along. He was special. Every chance she got, Jessica went into town, hoping to catch sight of him again. That was why she was afraid to talk about him, because she thought that if she did, she would jinx herself and then she'd never see him again.

"A friend of mine left it," Jessica mumbled, fitting the filter into place.

"A friend of yours?" Isabella's voice was shrewd. Jessica didn't have to look over to know that those gray eyes would be shrewd too. "You don't have any friends who are into classic cars. Unless you count that guy Winston with his Beetle."

"That's who it was," Jessica said quickly. "It was Winston."

"Jessica Wakefield!" Isabella grabbed her and pulled her so they were face to face. "You're lying! I can hear it in your voice. Come on, you can tell me. Whose magazine is it?"

Jessica was torn between the part of her that wanted to keep Michael McAllery a secret and the part that wanted to talk about him incessantly. The part that wanted to talk about him incessantly opened its big mouth.

"It's just this guy I ran into." Jessica made a face. "Actually, I ran into him literally. I bashed into his car when I was driving the Jeep."

Isabella leaned against the counter with a wicked smile. "And?"

"And not much," Jessica admitted. "He gave me a hard time when I hit him, but he never made a claim on the insurance. And then one day I came back to the room and he was lying on the couch, reading his magazine."

"What?" Isabella was still smiling, but her eyebrows shot up. "What do you mean, he was lying on the couch? How did he get in?"

"I don't know. He doesn't say much." Somehow, talking out loud about his behavior made it seem even weirder than it had before.

Isabella frowned. "Just who is this guy, Jess? Do you know his name?"

Jessica gave her an offended look. "Of course I know his name. It's Michael." At least his name was normal. You couldn't get any more normal than Michael.

"Not Michael McAllery," Isabella said.

Jessica looked at her sharply. "How did you know that?"

"There aren't that many mystery men around here who are into classic cars and good at picking locks." She made a face. "In fact, I'd say that Mike McAllery is probably it."

Jessica couldn't hide her excitement. "You mean you know him?" She grabbed Isabella's arm. "Tell me! Tell me everything you know. He isn't married or anything, is he?" She closed her eyes and groaned. "Oh, I knew it. I knew someone that gorgeous couldn't be unattached!"

"Hold on a minute, Jessica," Isabella said. "You're not actually interested in Mike, are you?"

There was something in Isabella's tone that Jessica didn't like—something serious—but she chose to ignore it.

"Interested?" she shrieked. "Are you kidding? How could I not be interested? He's the most incredible man I've ever met."

"He's gorgeous," Isabella agreed. "I'm not saying he isn't, but he's out of your league, Jess. Believe me. Michael McAllery is bad news."

"I don't believe it." Jessica took two mugs out of the drainer. "How can someone who looks like that be bad news?"

Isabella turned off the coffee maker. "How can someone who looks like that *not* be bad news?" She poured the coffee. "Really, Jess, this is not the kind of guy you want to get involved with. Mike McAllery left town right after high school because of some sort of scandal. I don't know if anybody remembers what it was, but it was huge at the time. Anyway, he went to L.A. and became a very successful photographer, and that was it. But then his father died a few years ago and he came back. He was the only child, and he inherited a fortune. But he's been in and out of trouble ever since. If it isn't drinking, it's women, and if it isn't women, it's fast cars."

Jessica felt herself go cold at the mention of women. "Maybe he's in mourning," she said. That would explain the drinking and running around. He hadn't gotten over his father's death.

"What?" Isabella started laughing. "Mike McAllery in *mourning*? For what?"

"For his father, obviously."

Isabella took a sip of coffee. "Oh, brother, do you have a lot to learn. Depending on who you hear it from, either Mike McAllery missed his father's funeral because he was out at the beach getting drunk, or because he was fooling around with his best friend's wife."

*It was grief,* Jessica told herself. *Isabella's wrong.*

*That's the way people act when they're overcome with grief.* "Those are just rumors," she said out loud. "People love spreading rumors about someone like that."

"Maybe." Isabella shrugged. "But I still think you should set your sights on someone a little more house-trained." She set her cup down. "I'll tell you what. Why don't I set you up with my friend Mark Gathers? He's a big basketball star and he's very dishy and very cool."

"Sure," Jessica said. "What's the difference? It isn't like Mike McAllery's interested in me or anything. I don't even know if I'd go out with him if he did ask me. He has been pretty rude."

"You should thank your guardian angel if he isn't interested in you," Isabella said. "She's saving you a load of trouble." She went over to the coffee table and picked up the student directory. "Now, let's just give Mark a call and see what he has to say for himself."

Jessica stared into her coffee cup. *Not only is Mike gorgeous and sexy,* she was thinking. *But he's misunderstood.* She smiled at her reflection in the dark liquid. Maybe their meeting had been destiny. Maybe she, Jessica Wakefield, was the one woman who could finally understand him.

The old Tom Watts had always done well enough in school, but he had been no scholar. If there was a choice between playing a little touch football and hitting the books, the old Tom Watts would have chosen running across a field with sweat streaking down his body any day of the week. What had mattered to him was being Wildman Watts, all-state champion and national record breaker, the college quarterback to watch. He could have anything he wanted; the world was his.

The new Tom Watts leaned back in his seat in the library study room, rubbing his eyes. The new Tom Watts knew that if there was something you wanted, you had to work for it; work hard and make it yours. He knew that the gifts the world gave you, the world took away.

Tom folded his arms on the tabletop and rested his head on them. He was tired. After his morning classes, he'd spent all afternoon and part of the evening at the university TV station. The station had become a huge part of his life. Tom didn't get into campus activities or the college social scene. He got A's in his classes, but it was without really participating, and the only friend he had was Danny. But he was involved in being an investigative reporter. That was what Tom Watts cared about: discovering the truth and making it known. He'd learned the hard way that fame and money and adulation were nothing to hold on to when things fell apart, but the truth was. The truth was one of the few things that might even be worth dying for.

Tom was drifting off into a half-dream where he

was tearing down a dark runway with a news camera over his shoulder when he was disturbed by a low, unpleasant male voice nearby.

"Well, whaddayaknow?" the voice was saying. "If it isn't Little Miss Equality."

Tom's eyes blinked open, and he felt his whole body tense.

A second male voice joined the conversation. "How about going to the movies with me some night, sweetheart?" it wheedled. "Or is this white girl reserved for black guys?"

"Hey, don't tell me you've gotten shy all of a sudden," said the first voice. "You had plenty to say at that Theta party."

"You're not very nice, you know," the other one said. "You don't stick up for your own kind, and you don't talk to them either. I think we're going to have to do something about that."

And then a girl spoke, her voice quiet but sharp. "Why don't you leave me alone?" she asked. "I'm trying to study."

Tom recognized her immediately. He remembered her voice so clearly and vividly that it seemed impossible he had heard it only once before.

"Because we think there's something you should learn here besides English." The taunting had become a threat.

"I'm serious. Go away."

"Oooh, I'm really scared . . ." They both laughed unpleasantly.

"What if we won't go away, honey? What are you going to do then?"

"She's not going to do anything." Tom barely spoke above a whisper, but the effect was as though he'd fired a gun. The two Sigmas had been bending down on either side of Elizabeth, but they straightened up immediately. Tom kept his eyes on them, not on the lovely face that had turned to him with relief.

"Hey, Watts," the larger one said. He smiled.

Tom didn't smile back. "I believe I heard Ms. Wakefield ask you to leave her alone," he said, his voice still hushed. "And I believe that would be a very good idea."

They both shrugged.

"Sure. Whatever."

"You're losing your sense of humor, Watts," the tall Sigma said. "We were just having some fun."

It wasn't until they'd left the study room that Tom finally looked at Elizabeth. For just a second their eyes met; and for just a second he thought about losing himself in them.

"Thanks," Elizabeth said.

The second passed. "Don't mention it," Tom said, and he turned his back on her and returned to his books.

"You guys watch too many soap operas," Jeff Cross was saying. "There's not going to be any bloodbath in Xavier Hall on Halloween. It's just a practical joke." He winked at Winston. "I wouldn't be surprised if old Win here had a hand in it."

Winston put down his coffee cup, shaking his head. "Not my style," he answered. "I'm strictly a jumping out of closets and impersonating the principal over the phone kind of guy."

A group of girls from Winston's dorm waved to him as they left the coffeehouse.

"You also seem to be the kind of guy who knows an awful lot of women," Bill said. "How did you meet so many so fast? You studying nursing or something?"

Winston smiled his new nonchalant, big-man-on-campus smile, while under the table he wiped his sweating palms on his jeans. No matter where he went with his Sigma buddies, he seemed to run into girls from his hall. He could hide in the men's bathroom and they'd find him.

"It's the old Egbert charm," he said. "Handed down from father to son." He put on a pained smile. "Believe me, guys, it's not a gift, it's a curse."

"Yeah, right." Andy Hoffer stuffed a last forkful of chocolate cake in his mouth. "You look like you're suffering."

*If you only knew,* Winston thought. His heart missed a beat as he noticed Candy and Anoushka walk through the door.

*Oh no, they're coming over!* He put a hand on his heart, less as a gesture of honesty than to keep it in his chest. "We Egberts are martyrs to our sense of duty," he managed to choke out as the girls approached.

Candy reached them first. She gave him a big, friendly smile. "Hi, Win—"

He couldn't let them call him Winnie. "Candy!" He got to his feet so quickly that he knocked his fork off the table. "Anoushka, great to see you! It's been a while."

Candy looked puzzled but smiled. "What are you talking about, we just saw you—"

Winston cut her off. "Do you guys know Candy and Anoushka?" He gestured to the Sigmas. "Candy, Anoushka . . . this is Bill, Andy, and Jeff."

"Hi," Candy and Anoushka said.

Winston wasn't the only person to be impressed by Candy's eyes and Anoushka's smile. The Sigmas were grinning back as though they'd been put in a trance.

Candy shook his arm. "We came over to ask you something."

Winston held his breath. *Please,* he silently begged. *Please don't let her ask if I still want to try her mango shampoo.*

"Debbie wanted to know if—"

Winston breathed again. Debbie wanted to know if she could borrow either his car, his weights, or one of his tapes. "Sure, sure," he said quickly, "tell her it's fine."

Candy was staring at him in bafflement. "Don't you even want to know what she wants?"

Winston started shoving the two of them along the aisle. "It's fine. Whatever she wants is fine."

"Hold on a minute, Win," Jeff said from behind him. "Why don't you ask your friends if they'd like to join us?"

Bill and Andy were both nodding.

"Yeah, there's plenty of room. You sit here; I'll get another chair,"Bill said to Anoushka.

"No! She can't." Winston gave Anoushka such a shove that she bumped into Candy. "They're very busy people," he went on, ignoring Candy's and Anoushka's strange glances. "They don't have time to eat; they're probably on their way to some important meeting or something . . ."

He knew he was gibbering, but he couldn't stop. "Maybe another time when they aren't in such a hurry." He grabbed Anoushka's elbow. "That would be nice, wouldn't it? We could all get together sometime for coffee when you and Candy aren't so busy . . ."

"What is wrong with you?" Anoushka shook him off. "Remind me to lend you some of my herbal relaxer when we get back to—"

The end of Anoushka's sentence was obliterated by the sound of breaking glass as Winston knocked a lemonade off a nearby table.

"Oh, I'm so sorry," he said, grabbing a napkin and mopping up the floor as Candy and Anoushka, with one last puzzled look, finally went away.

# Chapter Eight

*I've been on some boring dates in my time,* Jessica was thinking as Mark Gathers went through the lineup for the varsity basketball team, *but this has got to be one of the worst.* She was grateful that the coffeehouse was dark. As long as her face was in shadow she wouldn't have to pretend to be smiling the whole time.

She was so bored that the sight of Enid Rollins coming through the door actually cheered her up for a second. Jessica sat up straighter and tried to catch her eye. If she could get Enid to join them, at least she'd have someone to talk to. Enid's eyes fell on their table, and Jessica gave her a big smile. But instead of smiling back, Enid swung around and practically ran out the door.

*Maybe she's already met Mark and heard about the team,* Jessica thought. She looked back at Mark and felt guilty when she realized he thought she'd been smiling at him. The problem wasn't Mark. He was really a pretty nice guy; it was just that he wasn't Michael McAllery.

Somchow, as the days passed and she heard nothing from her mystery man, not being Mike McAllery had become something to hold against every other man on the planet. Whenever Jessica saw or talked to a guy, all she could think was, *He's okay, but he isn't Mike McAllery.*

"So, how are your classes?" Mark asked. Every few minutes he would notice the silence and make some comment about the university, or basketball, or the standard of food in the cafeteria, but the truth was, his mind seemed to be somewhere else too. "Are you taking anything you really like?"

She looked up at him. Mark was attractive. He was intelligent. He was a big basketball star and one of the most popular guys in the school. Jessica stifled a yawn. But he definitely wasn't Michael.

"It's okay," she said. "I like my music class." She didn't explain that the reason she liked music was that since they mostly listened to recordings, it gave her time to think about Michael.

Mark nodded. "Music," he said, fiddling with his coffee spoon. "Yeah, music's good."

Jessica nodded. "Yeah, it is."

Mark looked over at her, both worried and wary. "Look, Jessica, I know I'm a little distracted tonight, and I'd really like to apologize . . ."

She smiled blankly. "I'm having a wonderful time," she lied. "Really."

Mark smiled back, but his smile was rueful. "You don't have to be polite," he said. "This isn't exactly the date of the century. And I don't want you to misunderstand what I'm going to say, but the truth is that I came only as a favor to Isabella."

For the first time all evening, Jessica's attention was entirely focused on Mark. And she wanted to throw something at him. Every day another gorgeous guy was begging her to go out with him, but she turned them down. And for what? To go out with someone who "only came as a favor to Isabella"?

"Is this some new kind of line?" she asked coolly. "Wow her by making her think you don't like her?"

"I didn't mean that the way it sounded." He looked embarrassed. "All I meant was that though I *do* like you and find you very attractive, I'm actually interested in somebody else."

Jessica sipped her espresso. Although part of her was still annoyed, another part was grateful he'd let them both off the hook. "Well . . . to tell you the truth," she said as she put down her cup, "I'm interested in someone else too." She made a face. "I came only because Isabella wouldn't take no for an answer."

"Leave it to Isabella . . ." For the first time since he'd picked her up, Mark laughed a warm, genuine laugh. "What a relief, though. Now we can relax and have a good time. The group playing tonight's supposed to be really great."

Jessica picked up her bag. "Maybe I'll go to the ladies' room now, before the band starts."

"Good idea." Mark gestured to where some members of the basketball team were sitting. "I'll go say hello to the guys while you're gone."

Mark was still crouched between Todd and a guy Jessica didn't know when she came out of the rest room. Her eyes scanned the crowded room, looking for someone she knew. She spotted a guy from her science class . . . a girl who worked in the snack bar . . . a girl from her dorm . . . Jessica stopped suddenly. She felt as though a giant vacuum cleaner had sucked her heart right out of her chest. There, sitting on a stool at the counter, all by himself, was Michael McAllery. *He's not a student here,* she told herself. *Could he be following me?*

Afraid to move, Jessica watched as he lit a cigarette and exhaled a small cloud of smoke. When the cloud cleared, he was looking straight at her.

*He wants me to go over,* she decided, already walking toward him. *That's why he came tonight, to see me.*

She stopped only inches from him. After all these days and nights of imagining what it would be like to be kissed by him, being so close made her catch her breath.

"I knew I'd see you again," she purred in her sexiest voice, "but I didn't expect to see you here."

The gold eyes gave nothing away. "No?" Another cloud of smoke drifted around her.

She tossed her head. "No. I didn't think you'd be interested in this kind of scene."

"I'm not," he said. He pointed his cigarette at the tiny stage as the band started setting up. "The keyboardist is a friend of mine."

Jessica watched the keyboardist checking her amp. At that moment she looked up and winked in their direction. *He said friend,* Jessica reminded herself. *And that's what he meant, friend. He probably only came because it was an excuse to be on campus and run into me.*

"Oh." She wasn't quite sure what to say next. He wasn't exactly talking up a storm. "You know, I'd really love to take a ride in your car sometime," she said.

He glanced at her. "I think your boyfriend's wondering what happened to you," he answered, as though she hadn't spoken. He indicated Mark sitting at their table, looking around for her. She opened her mouth to explain that Mark wasn't her boyfriend, but he didn't give her a chance.

"You'd better sit down," he said. "The band's about to start."

"Am I the only person in this entire college who does any work?" Elizabeth threw down her pen and picked up the last cookie in the box as another song started on the stereo across the hall.

Shrieks of laughter rolled down the corridor. "They won't be laughing when they flunk out," Elizabeth told her desk lamp.

The door to the room opened suddenly, letting in more laughter and a blast of music. Elizabeth put her head on the desk. If Celine was already back, she'd never get her work finished.

"Is Celine here?"

Elizabeth looked up to find one of Celine's many friends, a large, loud girl who lived on the floor above, staring at her almost accusingly.

"She's on a date," Elizabeth said flatly. *Now just go away,* she added to herself.

But the girl didn't go away. Elizabeth watched in speechless amazement as she walked into the room, stepping over the pile of Celine's dirty clothes that had been left in front of the door.

"That's all right." The girl headed straight for Celine's dresser, rummaging around among the heap of makeup and toiletries on top. "I just wanted to borrow a couple of cigarettes." She held up a half-empty pack and stuck it in her pocket. "Tell Celine I'll pay her back tomorrow."

Elizabeth recovered her voice as the girl reached the door. "Maybe next time you could knock," she snapped. "I am trying to work."

The girl threw her a disgusted look. "They sure don't call you dull for nothing, do they?" she asked. The door slammed shut behind her.

Dull! Elizabeth could feel her face flushing with anger.

The music got louder as a second stereo joined the first. Dull! She wasn't dull, she was responsible. Let Celine, Jessica, Todd, and Alexandra throw all their energies into their social lives—she was going to do well in college. That's why she'd come, wasn't it?

Slamming her book shut, Elizabeth got to her feet. "That does it!" she shouted to the empty room. "I'm going to the library where I can concentrate."

As she steamed down the corridor, two girls carrying bags of chips and bottles of soda passed her.

"Where's *she* going?" one of them half whispered.

The other laughed. "Nowhere we'd want to be."

Tom stepped out of the television studio and into the night. His co-workers always joked that he was a workaholic. "You don't have to be here every spare minute," Professor Sedder, the head of the communications department, was always telling him.

He hurried across the quad. Sometimes he wondered if there might be some truth to the jokes. Especially now that Professor Sedder was threatening to get him a freshman trainee. "Even you can't do everything yourself," he'd told Tom that afternoon. "What happens if you get sick? What happens if NBC gives you a special award and sends you to Europe for a month?"

Tom looked at his watch. He'd arranged to

meet Danny for pizza half an hour ago.

He'd talked to enough psychiatrists and psychologists in the months right after the accident to know that he was overcompensating. "You think if you're always busy, you won't have to think about what happened," one doctor had told him. "But you're only fooling yourself."

Tom cut across the lawn, heading for the science building, where, hopefully, Danny was still waiting for him.

He wasn't fooling himself, though. Maybe he worked more than normal, but it wasn't because he was trying to stop himself from thinking about the accident. He never stopped thinking about the accident. Not a day went by that the memory of it didn't hit him like a sledgehammer. Not a night went by that it didn't replay itself in his dreams. It was with him every second of every minute of every twenty-four hours, and it always would be. He didn't work the way he did because he wanted to forget what had happened. He worked like that because he remembered; because he wanted to do something worthwhile with his life. It was his way of paying them back for what had been lost.

Tom slowed down as he noticed a girl with long, straight blond hair taking the library steps almost at a run. *Why is she always in there?* he asked himself. *Doesn't she have a room?* He stopped to watch her until she disappeared through the heavy oak doors. *Now what's* she *overcompensating for?* he wondered.

He might have stood there thinking about Elizabeth for the next hour if he hadn't spotted Danny, waiting under a palm tree. Danny was easy to pick out even from a distance or in a crowd because of his height and broadness. Tom waved.

Danny had just stepped onto the lawn when two figures came up behind him. One of them said something, and Danny stopped. *They probably just want to know the time,* Tom thought, but he stood up straighter, tense and watchful.

Danny started to walk again. One of the men reached out to grab his shoulder, but Danny was too fast. He kept walking, heading straight for Tom.

They were close enough now that even in the dim light, Tom could recognize them. One was Peter Wilbourne III, and the other was his yes-man, Simon Amerring. Their voices carried in the stillness of the night.

"What's the matter, Wyatt?" Peter was saying as they followed Danny. "You yellow as well as black?"

Simon found this pretty funny. Danny didn't say a word.

"He's just a lousy coward who needs some white guy to fight his battles for him!" Simon shouted.

Tom held himself in check. It wouldn't help Danny if he stepped in now.

Though they continued to taunt and poke at Danny, they stopped short of actually attacking him. Tom could only guess that Wilbourne and Amerring, aware of Danny's strength, weren't quite sure how far they could push him. They had to know that if he wanted to, he could take on the two of them without any trouble.

As soon as Danny approached, Tom stepped away from the building and walked beside him.

"I'm sorry I'm late," he said, acting as though he didn't know the white guys were behind Danny, as though he didn't know what had been going on.

"It's all right," Danny said. "I figured you lost track of time."

He could hear the Sigmas drop back as they came out onto the lighted path.

Tom glanced at his friend. Even though he'd sworn to himself that he'd never ask, there were times when he couldn't help wonder why. Why did Danny let those idiots push him around like that?

"You think I'm a coward too?"

Danny's voice was so normal, and the question so surprising, that for a second Tom wasn't sure he'd heard him right. "What?"

"Do you think I've gone soft?" Danny came to a stop under a streetlamp and turned to face him. "Come on, I know you must've thought about it. Why do you think I won't fight anymore?"

"Of course I've thought about it." Tom jammed his hands into his pockets, but looked straight into Danny's eyes. "It doesn't matter, man. You don't have to explain yourself to me."

"I know." Danny shrugged. "Maybe that's why I will."

Tom didn't interrupt him once. The two of them stood on opposite sides of the streetlamp, looking out across the campus, and Danny told him about his brother. His big brother, Thad.

All his life, Danny had looked up to Thad and tried to emulate him. Thad was a leader, so Danny became a leader. Thad was a fighter, so Danny became a fighter. "Don't let anybody push you around," Thad always told him. "Not anybody." And Danny didn't. But last winter, Thad had taken things a little too far. He'd gotten into an argument with some guys from L.A., and one of them had a knife.

"So now he's in a wheelchair for the rest of his life," Danny said. "It was a stupid argument, Tom. A stupid argument over parking a car. None of them could even remember how it started." He shook his head. "Can you figure that out? A stupid argument over a car, and now Thad will never walk again. I never thought something like that could happen," Danny said, his voice as dead as his brother's legs. "But now I think about it all the time."

"There are some things that are worth fighting for," Tom said, his eyes still on the moon. "But not that many."

"No," Danny said. "Not that many at all."

It was after midnight when Elizabeth followed the path back to Dickenson Hall. Exhausted, but relieved to have finished her work, she looked for a crack of light under the door of her room. It was dark. As late as it was, she knew Celine probably wasn't in bed. Celine slept so little at night and so much during the day that Elizabeth sometimes seriously wondered if she might be a vampire. Elizabeth slowly opened the door. *And she certainly has a taste for blood,* she thought ruefully, remembering the fight they'd had that morning.

Elizabeth crossed to her desk and turned on the light. Celine's bed was unmade, as usual, and empty. She threw down her books with a sigh of relief. All she wanted to do was get into her own bed and sink into a deep sleep before the Vampire Queen came home. She sat down for a minute before getting into her pajamas, just to relax. She kicked off her shoes. She closed her eyes.

"All work and no play makes Elizabeth a real bore," Jessica was saying. "That's why I didn't want to room with you, Elizabeth, because you're just so *dull.*"

"I'm not dull!" Elizabeth shouted back. She was standing in the center of a ring of people. Besides Jessica, Celine, Todd, and Alexandra, there were a bunch of Thetas and Sigmas. Everyone was pointing at her. "I'm very interesting. I—I'm—"

"No, you're not!" Alexandra shouted as the circle started skipping around her. "You're a boring old prude."

"I'm not!" Elizabeth was near tears, spinning around, trying to keep up with them.

"Little Goody Two Shoes," Celine drawled. "You're about as much fun as my granny's dentures." She laughed.

"Not everything in life has to be fun," Elizabeth protested.

Loose, high-pitched giggling rose above the taunting. Someone put a spotlight on Elizabeth.

"Look at her!" shrieked Celine in a loud whisper. "She even looks boring when she's sleeping."

A boy laughed. Elizabeth turned, trying to see who it was.

"Shhh!" Celine hissed. "You'll wake it up."

"We're going to wake it up anyway," the boy spluttered. Something thudded to the ground.

Shielding her eyes against the light, Elizabeth turned again and again, but the ring was fading.

"Maybe we should turn off the lamp," the boy whispered.

"I've got a better idea," Celine said between giggles. "Bombs away!"

Something soft and warm and smelling of tobacco fell over Elizabeth's head.

She opened her eyes to darkness and laughter. There was something over her face. She could smell whisky as well as tobacco. *I'm awake,* she told herself. *I'm awake, the light is on, and there's someone else in the room.* She flung Celine's sweater from her head and sat up, blinking.

Celine and a strange boy were sitting in a heap in the middle of the floor. Celine, her makeup smudged and her hair tousled, was slumped against him, her arms around his neck. Even in her dazed state, Elizabeth knew where the smell of liquor was coming from.

"Uh-oh," said Celine in a stage whisper. "I think we've been caught."

*Don't let them get to you,* Elizabeth told herself, grateful that at least she wasn't in her pink pajamas.

She got to her feet with as much dignity as she could muster. "Get this guy out of here, Celine," she ordered.

Celine struggled to a sitting position, hanging on to her date. "He's not going anywhere, Little Miss Priss! He's staying here tonight."

"In *my* room?"

Celine staggered to her feet. "It's my room, too," she yelled. "I can have whoever I want stay."

Someone from the room next door pounded on the wall. "Shut up! We're trying to get some sleep."

"Well, we're not!" Celine screamed back. "And we'll make as much noise as we want!" She slid back to the floor, her arms around the boy again. "Won't we, honey?" she asked.

Elizabeth was already out the door, her bag and her jacket in her arms, and didn't hear his reply.

Blind with tears, Elizabeth raced out of the dorm. She didn't care how much noise she made, she just wanted to get as far from room 28 and Celine as she could.

It wasn't until the front door of the building locked behind her that she stopped abruptly, gasping for air. What was she doing? Where could she go? The night was cold now; cold and moonless with only a scattering of stars.

*I'll go to Todd's,* Elizabeth told herself, pulling on her jacket. She started up the path, but the farther she got into the darkness, the less this seemed like a good idea. What if he wasn't there? Or, worse, what if he was and didn't want her around? She didn't even want to consider the possibility that he wasn't alone. She slowed down. It had been so long since they'd really spent any time together she couldn't be sure of her welcome anymore.

The image of her sister flashed through her mind, but she couldn't be sure of her welcome there, either. She imagined barging in on Jessica and her new crowd, her clothes rumpled and her face streaked with tears. She could hear Jessica saying, *Oh, grow up, will you, Elizabeth? We're in college now. It's no big deal to have a guy stay in your room one night.*

Something scurried through the bushes. Elizabeth picked up speed again. *Enid,* she decided. *I'll go there. No matter what's happened in the last few weeks, she'll be there for me. She's still my best friend.*

Almost running now, Elizabeth headed toward Enid's dorm. Memories of all the times Enid had stood beside her and comforted her filled her mind as she raced across the lawn.

But when Elizabeth finally got to Enid's dorm, she realized she'd made another mistake. Enid wasn't here. The Enid she'd been hurrying to no longer existed. The girl whose light shone through a third-floor window of Parker Hall was someone else. Someone called Alexandra who was pledging the most popular sorority, who had no time for Elizabeth anymore—someone who might have a guy in her own room tonight.

Elizabeth shivered. Except for the occasional campus patrol car passing by, she might have been the only person left on the grounds.

She turned away from the dorm and headed toward town. There must be an all-night laundromat or even a diner where she could sit until morning.

It was only as she reached the outskirts of town that she realized that there was in fact one person from her old life who wouldn't turn her away. A responsible, kind, caring, and generous person who lived in an off-campus apartment only a block or two from where she was now.

"Steven!" Why hadn't she thought of him before? Steven would help her. Steven would make her feel as comfortable and loved as she used to feel.

Elizabeth ran to her brother's, almost feeling as though she were going back to Sweet Valley, going home.

* * *

"What are you doing here? What's wrong?" Steven was standing on the landing, the door to his apartment open behind him, wearing a T-shirt and a pair of old sweatpants that had obviously been thrown on quickly, since they were inside out.

Elizabeth didn't care. She'd never been so happy to see anyone in her life. "Oh, Steven," she sobbed, hurling herself into his arms. "I've had the most terrible night."

"What is it?" a soft, gentle voice asked. An equally soft and gentle hand touched Elizabeth's shoulder. "What happened?"

Elizabeth pulled herself away from her brother's embrace. Steven's girlfriend, Billie, was standing beside them in the doorway, a robe pulled around her, her feet bare. Elizabeth had been so upset that she'd forgotten about Billie. She wiped the tears from her eyes and forced a smile. "It's nothing," she apologized, trying to keep her voice from wobbling too much. "I'm really sorry for bothering you. I . . . it's just . . ."

As the tears streamed down Elizabeth's face, both Steven and Billie slipped their arms around her and steered her into the apartment.

"Why don't I fix us all a cup of tea?" Billie asked. "Would you like that, Elizabeth? Some tea and cookies?" She gave her a squeeze. "It'll give you a chance to talk to your brother," she added in a whisper.

Elizabeth collapsed onto the sofa. Across from

her the bedroom door was open, the bed unmade, clothes thrown on the floor. She must have interrupted Steven and Billie; they'd obviously already gone to bed. Suddenly Elizabeth felt like an intruder. Why hadn't it occurred to her that her brother would be busy too? That he had his own life and it didn't include her?

Steven sat down beside her, resting one arm along the back of the couch. "What is it, Elizabeth?" he asked.

In the kitchen, Billie turned on the faucet to fill the kettle. "You take milk, Elizabeth?" she called.

Steven answered for her while Elizabeth snuffled back tears. He moved a little closer. "Come on, Elizabeth, tell me what's wrong."

Was it concern she heard in his voice or impatience? *Oh, stop it,* she scolded herself. *Of course it's concern. He's your brother. Just because he has a girlfriend doesn't mean he's stopped caring about you.*

Haltingly and in a voice choked with sobs, Elizabeth told Steven what had happened. But because she could hear Billie opening cabinets and getting out cups, and because she could still see the waiting bedroom out of the corner of her eye, she didn't talk about anything but Celine and her date.

Billie came in just as she'd finished, setting a tray filled with steaming mugs and a plate of chocolate-chip cookies on the coffee table.

Elizabeth caught the look Billie gave Steven. It was the sort of look she and Todd might have exchanged when they were close. It said, *Well? What's wrong?*

Steven started explaining as he handed Elizabeth her tea. "Elizabeth's roommate came back drunk with a guy tonight and refused to make him leave."

Billie sat beside Steven, leaning against him. "Oh, you poor thing," she said. "I know exactly what it's like, believe me. The first girl I shared with when I came here was like that." She laughed. "It got so bad that one time I actually barricaded the door so I could get a whole night's sleep."

Steven passed her the plate. "I think this is part of what they call the college experience," he said. "I could tell you stories about some of the people I've roomed with that would curl your hair."

Elizabeth smiled weakly, helping herself to a cookie. All of a sudden she was starving. "I know—" she began, hoping to explain that it wasn't just Celine that had her upset, that everything about college was wrong for her, that her entire life seemed to be falling apart.

But Steven cut her off. He started telling her a story about a roommate of his who used to bring his friends in through the window at all hours of the night to play cards and drink beer.

Elizabeth ate while Steven talked and Billie tried to keep her eyes open.

*What he's telling me is that it's no big deal,* Elizabeth thought. *What he's saying is that I'm overreacting and I should go back to my room.*

When Steven had finally finished his story and she'd finished her tea, Elizabeth put down her cup. "I guess I'll go now," she said, getting to her feet. "I'm really sorry I bothered you. I'm feeling much better now."

She turned to Steven just in time to see Billie nudge him.

"You don't have to go," he said quickly. "You can sleep here. We have a spare room."

Elizabeth shook her head. "No, it's all right. I have an exam first thing in the morning, anyway."

With a look at Billie, Steven stood up too. "I'll drive you back."

After Steven let her off, Elizabeth went back to Dickenson Hall, but not to room 28. Instead she went into the common room and huddled in one of the armchairs, dozing fitfully and wondering how the world had started moving so fast that it seemed to have left her behind.

# Chapter Nine

*It's not really true that I have no friends,* Elizabeth consoled herself as she entered the study room. Since she came here every night, she'd begun to recognize the faces of the regulars. At the front carrel was Nina Harper, a girl from her floor at Dickenson. The man who had come to her aid the night the Sigmas were hassling her—Tom something—was sitting to one side, and behind him was a pale, sharp-featured guy with longish blond hair who often stayed late reading books of poetry.

Maybe they weren't technically friends, but just seeing these people made her feel she wasn't completely alone. She smiled at Nina as she passed her desk, and Nina smiled back.

*Maybe I'm not the only one with roommate problems,* Elizabeth thought. She had to go almost to the back to find an empty carrel. As she walked up the aisle, she could feel the ice-blue eyes of the blond boy on her face. Sometimes, walking across campus, she would feel someone watching her and look up to find it was him. Elizabeth couldn't decide whether she liked this attention. Before she came to college, she would have thought nothing of an attractive guy noticing her, but her confidence was so low now she wasn't sure what it meant. She tried never to let him catch her looking back.

It was Tom's nod she responded to as she walked by. They hadn't spoken since he'd stepped in for her with the Sigmas, but they always acknowledged each other. And sometimes, when she looked into his face, she felt as though he really could be a friend.

Elizabeth chose a carrel behind Tom. *My home away from home,* she thought as she sat down. Her relationship with Celine had deteriorated rapidly after the night she'd fled the dorm. She and Celine never said a word to each other. Not one. Sometimes Elizabeth would come into the room and find Celine deep in conversation with one of her friends, but as soon as they saw her they clammed up. She figured they couldn't *always* be gossiping about her.

She took her pens, a notebook, and a chocolate bar out of her bag and began to go through her notes. A flier fell out from between the pages. It was for the big Halloween dance. COME TO THE ZOMBIE BALL! it said. BRING THE GHOUL OF YOUR CHOICE! Elizabeth jammed the paper back into her notebook. Todd hadn't asked her yet. Maybe he thought she wouldn't want to go, because of all the rumors about the psychopath.

Elizabeth sighed. Or maybe he thought she wouldn't want to go with him. If she did, what would she go as? A wallflower? A letter stamped return to sender? The invisible girl?

Something made her turn around to catch another glimpse of the man with the high cheekbones and the piercing stare. If he went to the party, he would probably go as Dracula. She could easily picture him in a black cape and a blood-red tie. *Which means that Celine, Vampire Queen, would be his perfect date.* Even as the thought crossed her mind he looked up again, his eyes almost seeming to reach out and catch hold of hers. Blushing, she turned back to her work.

Anoushka made a serious face at her reflection in the bathroom mirror. "You know what I think?" she asked, her eyes shifting to glance at Winston painfully shaving himself. "I think you should go to the Halloween dance as a girl."

Winston winced as the razor took off more than whiskers. "I may have to go as the victim of a brutal murder if you don't shut up and let me shave in peace."

"Oh, don't get touchy. I'm serious." She turned, looking at him closely. "You've got the right kind of face for it, and you must have picked up a lot about being a girl from living in Oakley."

"I won't argue with that," Winston answered. "I know so much about feminine-hygiene products I could probably walk out right now and get a job selling the stuff."

"You just have no sense of humor sometimes, do you?" She scooped up some water from the sink and splashed him. "I think it'd be great if you went in drag. You could go with me and Debbie; we don't have dates. I bet everybody would wonder why you weren't wearing a costume."

Winston put down his razor and turned to face her "Anoushka," he said in a patient voice. "Do you think you're bolstering my sense of self by saying I'd make a good woman? Do you? Because if you do, you're wrong. You're undermining my sexual identity."

"Oh, please . . ." She pulled out the plug.

Winston dabbed at his bleeding neck with a tissue. "You wouldn't catch me dressing up as a girl on Halloween, not when everybody's saying a psychopath's going to be on the loose."

Anoushka scooped up her things. "Why not?"

"Why not? Don't you read the papers?" Winston looked at her in the mirror. "Because most serial killers go for women."

She slapped him on the rear with her towel as she headed out the door. "In that case, maybe I'm the one who should go in drag."

"Alexandra! Alexandra, over here!"

Enid stood at the entrance to the stands, her eyes moving across the noisy crowd of students.

Delia nudged her. "Up there! See? Where that big Get 'Em Vanguards banner is."

Enid found the banner, and beneath it a large group of Thetas and their boyfriends. "Alex! Come sit with us!" one of the Thetas was shouting.

*Why are you hesitating?* Enid told herself. *The Thetas are calling you. You've done it! You've completely changed your image.* But her eyes continued to wander across the fans who had come to cheer on the Sweet Valley football team, the Vanguards, in their first home game.

Enid knew why she was hesitating. Because Jessica Wakefield was sitting at the end of the group and because Mark Gathers was nowhere around. She'd seen them together in the coffee house a few nights ago, and it had upset her so much that she'd turned around and left immediately. If Mark preferred Jessica, there was nothing she could do about it, but still she scanned the stands, searching for the guys from the basketball team, half hoping Todd might spot her and call to her to join them.

"Alexandra Rollins!" Delia hissed at her. "If you don't start moving, I'm going to drag you up there."

Enid knew when to give in. There wasn't any point in trying to avoid Jessica just because she'd gone out with Mark. Jessica was as likely to be pledged to the Thetas as Enid was. If they were going to be sorority sisters, they would at least have to pretend to get along.

Enid laughed. "Okay, okay."

"Now remember," Shaun said as they climbed the stairs. "I sit next to the guy in the blue sweater if humanly possible."

"That's fine with me," Delia said. "I've got my eye on one of the Vanguards." She made a face. "I just wish I could remember what his number is. It's pretty hard to tell them apart with their helmets on."

"So, what does everybody think?" Enid said with a big smile as she squeezed into a seat beside Kimberley Schyler and her boyfriend, Tony. "Are we going to wipe the field with them or what?"

Tony shook his head. "We'll be lucky if they don't wipe the field with us," he said. "Our team hasn't been the same since Watts quit."

Enid nodded, squinting at the end of the bleachers, hoping for a glimpse of a familiar face.

"Oh, come on," the guy sitting behind Tony said. "It's not that bad. Watts was a genius, but we've still got some good players."

Kimberley groaned. "Give us a break, you two. Alexandra doesn't want to hear about the legend of Wildman Watts and how the future of the Vanguards was ruined the day he quit the team."

"Yes, I do," Enid said, even though she was a lot more interested in basketball players than football players at the moment. "Who was this guy Watts? What happened to him?"

Nick smiled at her in a way that reminded her that she really wasn't Enid anymore. "Tom Watts was a phenomenal quarterback. He made himself a legend in his freshman year, and then he just dropped out completely."

"You mean from football?"

Tony shrugged. "From football, from his friends . . . from everything."

"Where is he now?" Enid half expected them to say he'd gone to live in the desert by himself.

Nick pointed to the field. "Down there," he said. "With the camera. All he does now besides go to classes is work for the campus TV station."

"The regular guy must be sick or something," Tony put in. "Tom's a reporter, not a cameraman."

Nick put his head close to hers. "You see him? The big guy in the black shirt?"

Enid nodded, but she didn't see Tom Watts at all. Far away as he was, she had suddenly recognized the man standing beside the cameraman, talking and nodding. It was Mark.

She sucked in her breath. *This is my chance,* she thought. *Somehow or other, I have to talk to him before the end of this game.*

"See who I mean?" Nick was still pointing.

"Oh, yes," Enid said, her eyes on Mark. "I see."

"It can't just be a story," Denise was saying. "There are too many details. The psychopath will be dressed in black. He'll use a knife. The first victim will be a beautiful blonde . . ."

The guy she was talking to, Ben Somebody, groaned in exasperation. "Cripes, Denise, those aren't details; they're the little extras people put in every time they tell the story again."

Denise gave him a withering look. "Oh, sure. And I suppose naming Xavier Hall as the site of the murders is a little extra too."

Ben ran his hand through his hair in exasperation. "But that's just it," he argued. "Whoever started these stupid rumors chose Xavier Hall because it would make the stories seem real."

Jessica had been half listening to this conversation while she idly scanned the bleachers for a familiar face, but the only one she'd found was "Alexandra" Rollins's. How ironic could you get? Here she was at her first college football game. She wasn't on the cheerleading team yet because they'd had only two openings, and she was sitting with a group dominated by Enid the Drip.

She turned to Denise. "Well, it worked, then. Everybody believes something horrible is going to happen at the Halloween dance." She yawned. "That's all anybody talks about anymore."

Denise laughed. "Don't tell me Jessica's bored," she teased. "Are serial killers so commonplace in your part of Sweet Valley that you're already tired of ours?"

"It's not that we have that many psychopaths."

Jessica smiled sweetly. "It's just that we don't talk about them so much."

Ben laughed. "I'm with Jess. I'm sick of everybody talking about the Halloweeen Horror all the time. If they're that worried, then cancel the dance."

*"Cancel the dance?"* Both Denise and Jessica stared at him as though the killer had suddenly materialized behind his head.

"Are you crazy?" Jessica demanded. "Cancel the dance just because of a little bloodbath?"

Denise gave him a shove. "This is the first big social event of the year, you moron. Nobody's going to cancel it just because of a few rumors."

Ben shook his head. "Women," he muttered. "I wish I could understand them." He shrugged. "But since I can't, I think I might fight my way down to the snack van. Anybody want anything?"

Jessica was about to say no when she suddenly felt her heart drop into her stomach. The one thing she did want was disappearing out the exit two aisles away.

*Mike!* She got to her feet so fast she knocked Ben back into his seat. "I'll get it," she said quickly. "I have to go to the ladies' room anyway."

"That's all right, Jess—" he began, but she climbed right over him.

"Hot dog?" she asked, backing down the stairs. "Fries? Soda?"

As she raced toward the exit she heard Ben call after her, "Two large fries and a cheeseburger!"

With the determination of an explorer, Jessica fought her way through the crowd to the refreshment vans parked behind the stadium. What if he wasn't there? What if he wasn't going for food? What if he was leaving?

*Don't be silly,* she told herself as she shoved several people out of her way. He didn't buy a ticket just to leave before the game even started.

But Michael McAllery wasn't buying food. She pushed on. He wasn't in line for the men's room, either. Jessica stopped. There wasn't anywhere else he could be. He really must have been leaving. She looked around as the crowd began to thin out. The game would be starting soon. She might as well give up and go back to her seat.

"What's the matter, blondie?" asked a voice directly behind her. "Did you forget where you're sitting?"

Jessica was so surprised that she jumped.

Michael McAllery was standing so close to her, she could smell the soap he'd used that morning. He was grinning at her.

"What's the matter?" he asked, his voice unusually gentle. "Did you think I was the psychokiller, making an early appearance?"

Jessica gazed up at him. "I'd think you'd be more the type to save me from him," she said, pouting sexily. "I didn't think I was in danger from you."

He reached out and twisted a strand of her

golden hair between his fingers. "Don't kid yourself, sweetheart," he whispered. "You're always in danger from me."

Todd glanced at his watch again. What had happened to Mark? He'd gone for sodas at the beginning of halftime, and now the second half was about to start and he still hadn't come back.

"Well, hello, stranger," said a voice sweeter than honey and twice as smooth. "You saving this seat for me?"

Todd turned. It was Celine, dressed in something tight and blue-green, her hair and eyes and lips all sparkling in the sun.

"Sure," he said immediately, shifting over. "Sit down." Now he found himself hoping that Mark wouldn't come back after all. "You just get here?"

Celine squeezed in next to him. "No, I've been here since the beginning." She pointed toward the field. "I was down there with some of the girls from the dorm when I noticed you sitting here on your own." She held out a box of candy to him, smiling shyly. "If there's one thing I can't stand, it's a handsome man all by himself."

Todd blushed. He'd never met a woman who was so direct with a compliment. "I'm not supposed to be alone," he said. He meant that he was supposed to be with Mark, but Celine misunderstood him.

"Elizabeth is busy as usual?" she asked gently.

Something in the way she said "busy as usual" made him look at her closely. Todd had been under the impression that he was the one who was always busy, not Elizabeth. According to Elizabeth, all she ever did was study.

"Elizabeth had a paper to do today," he said. "I'm seeing her tonight."

"Oh, I'm so glad to hear that, Todd, I really am." She looked uneasily at the ground. "It's just that I do won—worry about Elizabeth, you know. She's never in our room anymore. She's gone by the time I wake up in the morning, and she doesn't get back until I'm already asleep." She sighed, looking up at him out of the corner of her eye. "Of course, I *know* she works in the library all the time, but you can understand why I'm concerned."

Todd couldn't exactly understand. "Well, Elizabeth has always been a very serious, hardworking person," he said. "She's always had her priorities straight, I guess."

Celine touched his wrist. "There are priorities and there are priorities. I was hoping that when Elizabeth said she couldn't come with us today, it meant she was coming with you." Her hand was warm and reassuring on his arm. "I guess things are different where I come from," Celine went on, her voice making him think of sultry nights and Spanish moss. "But I was raised to believe that a woman always makes time for her man."

He hadn't quite thought of it like that before,

but she was right. Ever since they'd gotten to college, Elizabeth had made no time for him, no effort. She wasn't happy about his success and popularity, and she certainly didn't want to share in it. What Elizabeth Wakefield wanted was to lock herself in the library.

Celine gently squeezed his arm. "It's like my granny always says, If you have no time to ride your horse, then maybe you shouldn't have one."

"Hey, Gathers!" Todd threw his towel across the bathroom. "What happened to you this afternoon? It's a good thing I wasn't waiting for you to bring back a doctor—I would've died."

Mark turned from the sink with a slightly shy smile. "I'm sorry, man, I really am. But I got sort of distracted at the snack bar."

Todd put his shaving kit down. "Oh, really? And do I need to ask by what?"

Mark's smile brightened. "No, but you might want to ask by whom."

Todd turned on the faucet. "Well, it's not Jess, I know that. You look too happy." He took another look at Mark, who had started shaving again. "Do I detect a hot and heavy date?"

Mark waggled his eyebrows in the mirror. "You do, my man. You definitely do. In fact, Wilkins, you may very well be watching a man preparing for the date of a lifetime."

Todd snapped his fingers. "Enid!"

"Alex," Mark corrected him. "The incredibly intelligent, beautiful, and sexy Alex Rollins." He rinsed his razor in the sink. "I can't believe how close I came to blowing it. Do you know, Alex *saw* me with Jess the other night?" He faced his friend. "What was I thinking, going out with someone else when I knew I wanted to be with her? Even as a favor, it was a stupid thing to do."

Todd laughed. "Did you two even bother to stay for the second half?"

Mark's good-natured grin returned. "We decided the coffee was better in the coffeehouse." He splashed water on his face. "What about you? You seeing Elizabeth tonight?"

Todd nodded, concentrating on putting lather on his face. Ever since that afternoon he'd been thinking about what Celine had said. "Yeah, we're having dinner together."

"Nice, Wilkins. I'll be sure not to barge in to tell you what a good time I had when I get back. But expect me right after breakfast."

*Don't worry about it,* Todd thought as he watched Mark saunter out of the bathroom. *You could bring the Marine marching band in with you and you probably wouldn't be disturbing us.*

It was wrong from the start. As excited as she was to be having a real date with Todd—and to be out of the room for the night and not in a carrel in the study room—Elizabeth was nervous about what to expect from the evening. As she walked across campus she couldn't shake the idea that what happened tonight might determine the fate of her and Todd's relationship forever.

What if after so many weeks of hardly speaking they couldn't find anything to talk about? What if, next to his new friends, he found her as dull as Jessica and Celine claimed she was? What if all his big-jock conversation annoyed her as much as it had before? What if he pressured her again?

And when he'd opened the door to his room, his body was so tense and his eyes somehow so suspicious that she'd immediately known she'd been right. It was going to be wrong.

"So," he said as she sat down in the armchair. "Did you get all your studying done?"

Elizabeth nodded. No matter which direction she looked, her eyes seemed to fall on the bed. "How about you? Was it a good game?"

Todd shook his head. "Not really. We lost twenty to zero." He handed her a glass of soda and sat down across from her. "Celine was there."

"Oh, really?" Her grasp tightened on the glass. "I didn't know you knew her."

Todd stretched his legs. "You know, Liz, in all honesty I don't know why you dislike Celine so much. She's really nice. She's sensitive, she's—"

"She's a two-faced witch." The words were out of her mouth before she'd realized they were even in her head.

Todd's expression was surprised and irritated. "Celine really likes you a lot, Liz. She's as concerned about you as I am."

"Concerned? You're concerned about *me*?"

Todd nodded. "Of course I am."

Elizabeth banged her glass down. "And how do you show this concern?" she demanded. "By talking about me behind my back to Celine?" The weeks of frustration and loneliness and feeling abandoned all rushed through her like a very fast train. "That's supposed to mean that ever since we've been here, you haven't paid as much attention to me as you pay to your basketball shoes."

"*I* haven't been paying any attention to *you*?" Todd got to his feet. "You're the one who hasn't been paying any attention to me. You won't even let me touch you."

She stood up too. "Since when does our relationship depend on how much I let you touch me? Since when does my not sleeping with you mean I'm not paying any attention to you?"

"That's not what I said!" he shouted. "Stop trying to put words in my mouth."

"All right!" she shouted back. "You tell me what you're thinking. You tell me what you want."

He collapsed on the bed, his head in his hands. It was such a sudden movement that she almost thought he was in pain. "All right," he said, his voice muffled. "All right, I'll tell you what I think." He raised his head, looking straight at her, his eyes full of sorrow. "I think this just isn't working. I think maybe it's time you and I went our separate ways."

*I'm okay,* Elizabeth told herself as she silently picked up her bag and her jacket. *Todd's right, it isn't working. It isn't working and it hasn't been working, and the quicker I get out of here, the better off we'll all be.*

Todd buried his face in his hands again. "I'm sorry, Liz. His voice was thick and muffled. "I'm really, really sorry."

Elizabeth didn't answer. She was already running down the hall, hoping to reach the safety of the elevator before the tears began.

"Isn't it a small world?" Celine asked. "Imagine us both ending up at the same school. I had no idea you went to SVU." She slipped her arm into the arm of the man beside her as they walked across the parking lot of Dickenson to his silver convertible Karmann Ghia.

"We're not walking on ice, Celine," he said, his voice itself like ice. "There's really no need to hold on to me."

Celine ignored his rudeness. If there was one thing she'd learned in her eighteen years, it was that you got nowhere in this life by doing as you were told.

"Don't be like that, William," she chided coyly. "After all, our families have known each other for generations. And we did have that date in New York last spring, didn't we?"

"You may call it a date, honeychile," he drawled, crudely imitating her accent. "But I call it an exercise in genteel blackmail." He came to a stop, extricated his arm, and opened the door.

A dark look came into Celine's face as she slid into the passenger seat. It was true that she'd had her father arrange for William White to be her escort to the debutantes' ball last June, but she hadn't realized at the time how much of an ordeal William had found it. He had been less than gracious, but then, he was a Yankee; she hadn't expected manners. It wasn't his manners that attracted her to him. It was his sensuous good looks and his slightly jaded, untamed air. Her instincts told her that he wasn't just unique and mysterious; he was dangerous. In fact, of the things that had made her choose SVU, William Barrington White's presence here was one of the most important. She'd been sure that once he realized she was nearby, he'd be all over her like flies on a picnic.

She was smiling again by the time he shut the driver's door. "Then what do you call this?"

He started the engine. "I call this a ride to the Sigma party." He put the car in reverse and backed out of the space. "And if I hadn't been so surprised that you had the nerve to ask me to take you, you can be sure that I would never have said yes."

Celine pushed back a tangle of curls. She wasn't

used to rejection, not from men. Men usually found her irresistible. She glanced over at William, his sharp, clear features, his piercing eyes, his longish blond hair. She was as attractive as he was, or nearly, and her family had just as much money as his. Why was he so impervious to her charms?

She ran her finger over the gearshift. "You know what I've always found amusing about you, William?"

"Don't touch, Celine." He pushed her hand away. "I know all about your weird sense of fun. One minute you're fondling the shift, and the next you're steering us into a ditch."

She leaned back, gazing up at the sky, her hair blowing around her face. "I've always thought it was amusing that your name's White, but you dress all in black."

They stopped at an intersection.

"Don't you think that's amusing, William?" she purred. She waited for his usual sarcastic response, and when it didn't come, she straightened her head. William was staring to the right.

"What's the matter?" Celine snapped. "Why aren't we going?"

"Shut up," he ordered. "Someone's coming."

She followed his gaze. Just reaching the crossing was a blonde in a prim, long-skirted white cotton dress. She didn't stop at the corner to check for traffic but hurled herself across the road.

"Oh, I don't believe it." Celine groaned. "It's

like being followed by your own tail."

William was now looking to the left. "What is?"

Celine pointed to the fleeing girl. "That is." She sighed melodramatically. "And of course she's crying. I have never seen one woman cry so much in my life."

For almost the first time since he had picked her up, William was looking at her. "You know that girl?"

Celine fished a cigarette out of her bag. "Of course I know her. I live with her." She struck her lighter. "If you want to call it living."

The car glided into motion again. "What's her name?"

Celine turned her head, her eyes as sharp as a cat's. Could it possibly be true? Had the handsome, wealthy, and enigmatic William White rejected *her* only to be interested in Little Goody Two Shoes? "Elizabeth," she answered tonelessly.

"And you're her roommate." He looked over at her. "I guess it is a small world after all," he said with a smile.

*I am going to get you for this, William White,* Celine decided. *Just you wait. I am going to make you fall in love with me if it's the last thing I do.* She blew smoke in his face. *And then I'm going to break your ugly little heart.*

# Chapter Ten

Jessica was sitting on the living-room floor, surrounded by sewing materials, hemming the skirt of her Halloween costume. She was amazed to discover that her classes weren't a total waste of time. After all, if it weren't for her freshman humanities course, she wouldn't have heard about the *Odyssey,* and she wouldn't have thought of going to the dance as Penelope.

She sighed, thinking once again of Mike McAllery—not that she thought about much else lately. Somehow Penelope, weaving by day and unweaving by night while she waited for the return of Odysseus, the husband she loved, seemed perfect. Penelope, like Jessica, was madly in love, steadfast and true. Like Jessica, she was separated from the man of her dreams by almost insurmountable obstacles. In Penelope's case a war; in Jessica's the fact that the man of her dreams wasn't particularly interested in her. But the best part about Penelope was that at the end of the story, she got Odysseus back.

Jessica leaned against the sofa, thinking about Penelope, running to meet her husband's ship, all her years of sacrifice and loneliness finally over. But when Odysseus stepped out on the deck, she saw Michael in black jeans and a rust-colored silk shirt, and instead of Penelope, she pictured herself running into his arms.

The ringing of the telephone disrupted the passionate kiss between her and Michael. Jessica's heart banged against her chest. Maybe it was him. *Don't be stupid,* she scolded herself as she reached for the phone. *You always think it's him and it never is.* She lifted the receiver, part of her still whispering, *Yeah, but maybe this time it really is.*

It was Steven. Her brother's voice was as warm and friendly as ever, but she knew him well enough to know after a few minutes that this wasn't just a casual call. Every time he finished one sentence, he started the next with "So." It was a dead giveaway.

"So," Steven said after she told him about her costume. "I saw you at the game the other day."

"Really?" She picked a piece of thread from the carpet. "Why didn't you come over and say hello?"

Steven's voice lost a little of its warmth. "You seemed pretty busy." He swallowed hard. "You were talking to Mike McAllery at the time."

The Jessica Wakefield early-warning system told

her that this was it. She kept her own voice casual. "I didn't know you knew Mike."

Usually her brother's laugh was a pleasant sound, but this one wasn't. "Jessica, everybody within a hundred-mile radius knows Mike McAllery. Especially if they're female or work for the police force."

Jessica stiffened. She'd had enough lectures from Isabella on the subject of Michael McAllery to be able to guess what was coming. "What are you trying to say, Steven? Is this your way of giving me a little brotherly advice?"

"I'll tell you exactly what I'm saying, Jess. Mike McAllery is bad news. He's wild, he's a womanizer, and though nobody's quite sure what he does for a living anymore, you don't have to be Einstein to figure out that he isn't selling Girl Scout cookies."

She was holding the receiver so hard that her hand was sweating. "What you're saying is that you know nothing about the man, but you've already judged him."

"No. What I'm saying is that you better stay away from him. This isn't advice, it's an order."

Enraged, she sat up on her knees, her face flushed. "You can't order me, Steven. I'm an adult now. I can see anybody I want."

"You may be an adult, but you're still my little sister!" He was shouting now. "I'm not going to sit back and watch you throw yourself at a piece of scum like Mike McAllery."

"How dare you!" She'd always been able to shout louder than he could. "How dare you say that! You don't even know him. You're just jealous because you could never be the man he is."

"I wouldn't want to be the man he is!" Steven shouted back. "And I don't want him hanging around my sister."

"Well, that's just too bad, isn't it?" she thundered. "Because, really, Steven, there isn't one little thing you can do to stop it." She slammed the phone down so hard that it fell off the table.

Jessica slumped against the couch, tears of rage filling her eyes. It wasn't bad enough that Mike didn't want her. Nobody wanted her to want him. She reached into the magazine rack and took out the one he'd been reading the day she found him lying on the couch and held it against her. "I'm not giving up," she said out loud. "I don't care what anybody says. I'm not giving up." Another small gray rectangle of paper fell out. Wiping her eyes on the sleeve of her blouse, she reached down and picked it up. How had she missed this the first time? It was his card. *Michael McAllery, 555-4343.*

"I don't believe this," Jessica whispered. "I've had his number all the time. He left it for me!" All the unhappiness and anger were instantly replaced with euphoria.

Holding the card against her heart, Jessica sank into the couch. "You just try and keep me away from him, Steven Wakefield," she said. "You just try."

* * *

Tom was bent over the editing table, doing the rough cut of his feature about the psychic's predictions for Halloween night. He was dimly aware that the snack bar and the coffeehouse had been decorated with orange and black streamers and jack-o'-lanterns. He'd even noticed the paper skeletons in the cafeteria and the black cat taped to the door of his dorm. In classes he overheard people talking about masquerade parties and the Halloween dance, but none of that really meant anything to him. All Halloween meant to him was the final chapter in his mini-documentary: *What Happened That Night.*

Tom leaned back, rubbing his eyes. He was pleased with what he had so far. He'd interviewed the psychic, Barnabas Montoya, and several people who regularly consulted him, including the chief of police. Then he'd done an overview of the campus, intercutting interviews with students in which he'd asked them whether or not they believed the predictions, and ending with Tom himself standing in the empty gym of Xavier Hall, wondering what October 31 might bring.

He ran a hand through his hair. With a little luck, he might even get one of the local stations to pick up his story. "Some luck," he muttered to himself as he slid off his chair in search of a cup of coffee. "Guaranteed a local will take it if something awful does happen."

Not that Tom thought anything was going to happen. He'd spoken with a lot of people, and as far as he could tell, old Barnabas was no more than your average lucky guesser—and not always that. Tom had a hunch that the psychic was trying to drum up a little extra business for himself. In fact, when Tom actually sat down and talked to Montoya, his predictions for Halloween night were a lot more vague than those of the students at Sweet Valley University.

All over the campus people were saying that the killer would carry a knife, that his first victim would be a beautiful blonde, and that he'd strike just before midnight. One kid Tom talked to even described the psychopath in detail, saying he'd be dressed all in black with a black ski mask over his face. "What color shoes?" Tom had asked, but the kid hadn't seen the joke.

No one else saw the joke, either. They were all too busy egging each other on. That was why he'd wanted to do the documentary, to show how rumors get started and take on a life of their own.

Tom stared thoughtfully into his steaming mug of coffee. Doing the edit, he'd realized there was something about the whole business that was disturbing him in a real way, but he couldn't quite put his finger on what it was. Just a feeling. He didn't believe in Barnabas Montoya's killer, but he did believe something was going to happen—something nasty.

When Tom separated the actual prediction from the fantastic stories that had built up around it, there was one strand of rumor that gave him a chill. The blonde. Barnabas swore he'd never said anything about victims at all, but everyone had heard about the beautiful blonde. And no one remembered exactly where.

Tom put down his coffee and went back to the editing board. Maybe it was because when he thought of the blonde, he thought of Elizabeth Wakefield, but it disturbed him that this one detail should be so specific.

Tom glanced at his watch. He didn't have much time. Professor Sedder, the station adviser, had arranged for him to spend the rest of the afternoon training the new intern who had been recommended by the English department.

He hadn't even bothered to disguise his anger about this. "I can't believe we're getting a freshman," Tom had raged. "How can you expect me to waste my time training a freshman? Are you crazy? We hardly ever take on even sophomores." But Professor Sedder wasn't interested in Tom's complaints. He'd had the assurance of the head of English that this guy was really hot, a seasoned journalist with real style and flair.

Soon Tom was deep in his work again, his worries about blondes and his complaints about freshmen forgotten. He was so engrossed that he didn't know someone had come into the room until he felt a hand on his shoulder.

"Geez!" he snapped. "Why don't you knock?"

"I'm sorry," said a delicate female voice. "I didn't mean to startle you. Professor Sedder said I should just come in."

Tom turned around. And found himself staring into the beautiful blue-green eyes of Elizabeth Wakefield.

She smiled, and it was as though someone had turned up the lights. "It's you!" she said.

"You took the words right out of my mouth," Tom answered.

Elizabeth was in a good mood as she hurried back to the dorm, the package her mother had sent her tucked under her arm. In fact, she was in a great mood—the best she'd been in for weeks. And she had Tom Watts to thank. Since she'd started working with him at the TV station, she'd rediscovered the excitement she used to feel working on the *Oracle*, the Sweet Valley High paper.

*How could I have forgotten how much I love reporting?* she wondered as she opened the door to her room. How could she have forgotten how nice it was to work with someone who was funny, intelligent, and as excited about a story as she was?

Elizabeth sat down on the bed to open the parcel. She hadn't planned to go to the Halloween dance, but she was feeling so much more confident these past few days she'd asked her mother to send her the costume she'd worn last year, just in case she decided to go after all.

She lifted out the multicolored silk skirt and peasant blouse. Gypsies weren't supposed to be blond, but she knew she looked good in this outfit. Todd had certainly thought so last year. She remembered him grabbing her and pretending to run off with her.

Elizabeth quickly shook off the memory and stepped into the silk skirt. Something was wrong; she couldn't get it to close. Elizabeth stared at herself in the full-length mirror. She gave another tug on the waistband.

"I don't understand it," she said to her reflection. "Last year it fit me fine." She tried holding in her stomach, but still she couldn't get it to fasten. "But I've always been a perfect size six," she wailed. *"Always."*

Elizabeth turned to the side. Not anymore. If she was a perfect anything, it was an eight. Maybe even a ten. Now that she was looking, she could see that her hips and breasts were a little heavier; even her cheeks seemed full. She felt like one of those Before and After photographs in a women's magazines. Only, she was becoming Before.

"It's misery," she told herself. "I've been comforting myself with cookies and potato chips." She twisted around to get a look at her bottom. No, she decided, she hadn't been comforting herself. She'd been eating herself into a coma.

Elizabeth faced the mirror again, wondering if crying burned up any extra calories.

"Gypsy," Elizabeth mumbled as she stepped out of the skirt. "If I go as anything, it'll be a pumpkin." She picked up the skirt, flung it into the bottom of her closet, and threw herself on her bed.

Something crackled beside her. She looked over and saw the half-empty box of peanut-butter cookies she'd been eating while she studied last night. A sudden pang of longing attacked her.

Elizabeth reached for the box. What was one little peanut-butter cookie? She wouldn't have any more after that. Ever. And tomorrow she'd think about going on a diet. But right now she needed something to make her feel better.

Just as she put the cookie to her lips, a voice inside her head started screaming. *Drop that! Have you completely lost your mind? If you hadn't eaten so many boxes of cookies in the last few weeks, you wouldn't need to feel better. You'd still be a size six!*

Elizabeth sat up. The voice was right. Tomorrow was too late to start her diet. She'd been letting herself slide since she got to college, and it was time she stopped. It wasn't until she'd started her internship at the television station that she realized how bored she'd been. She'd been burying herself in her classes, thinking that because she was busy she was all right.

But her afternoons with Tom Watts had made her realize she was wrong. The thrill she used to feel at *Oracle* meetings had come back to her, the buzz she got when she was working on a story.

Elizabeth put the cookie back in the box and stood up. Maybe it was time she faced things honestly. She tossed the box into the wastebasket.

Starting with her hips.

"But it doesn't make sense," Danny said over the din of the snack bar. "Why would the Sigmas start a rumor like that?"

Tom pointed a french fry at him. "You're the one who used to be a Sigma. You tell me."

Danny shook his head. "I can't. It doesn't make sense. When I was in the Sigmas, they were into climbing mountains and working out, not spreading psycho stories."

"When you were in the Sigmas, Peter the Horrible wasn't their president," Tom pointed out.

"You think that has something to do with it?"

Tom shrugged. He'd followed his feeling about the Halloween rumors and spent an afternoon in the cafeteria, asking everyone who came in what they'd heard and where. Most people had no idea, but a few of them said they'd heard about the blonde at a Sigma party. "If I'm right and it is the Sigmas who started all this, then you can bet Wilbourne's at the bottom of it."

Danny chewed thoughtfully on his burger. "If Wilbourne's at the bottom of it, then you can be sure it's not just a practical joke. You know what he's like. He did it for a reason, and you can bet your tape machine it won't be pleasant."

"You know him better than anyone." Tom picked up another fry. "You've outguessed him before. What do you think it could be?"

Danny laughed. "Well, that's easy. Peter only does anything for one of three reasons:ego, jealousy, or revenge."

"Ego, jealousy, or revenge," Tom repeated. "Now I just have to figure out which one it is."

"Sit still," Samantha ordered. "I can't do your eyes if you're wiggling." She shoved him back against the chair. "And stop blinking. You're going to be crooked."

Winston blinked as the eyeliner came toward him again. "You mean I'm going to be blind."

He couldn't understand how women put up with so much torture. So far he'd had his eyelashes curled, his eyebrows tweezed, his nails manicured—he felt as though he'd spent the last two hours on the rack. He'd always thought that women went to beauty parlors to relax and indulge themselves; now he realized they went to toughen up in case they were ever made prisoners of war.

Candy looked up from the sink, where she was putting her manicure set away. "Those nails are still tacky, Win. Don't go getting fluff on them."

"Winnie!" Debbie kneed him in the back. "Will you please relax? If I don't get this wig combed out right, you're going to look more like Harpo Marx than Shirley Temple."

"The only way I'm going to relax while Samantha's trying to dig my pupils out is if you knock me unconscious."

Shirley Temple had been the Sigmas' idea—and his dormmates had immediately taken it to their hearts. They all thought Shirley Temple was really cute. It could have been worse, he supposed. One of the other Sigma hopefuls had to go as Marilyn Monroe. At least Shirley Temple didn't wear heels.

"Men . . ." Debbie sighed. "You really are overly delicate, aren't you?"

"You mean they really are babies," said Candy.

"We are not babies," Winston said, trying hard to keep the pain out of his voice. Why did he spend half his time defending the entire male sex? "We're just not raised for self-mutilation, that's all."

Candy laughed. "No, guys like mutilating other people instead."

The bathroom door flew open with a bang. "I found it!" Anoushka came charging into the room. "I knew I had it somewhere."

"Watch it!" Winston whimpered as Samantha started glueing his lashes together.

This time she kicked him. "Sit still, Win. It wouldn't hurt if you'd cooperate a little."

"Sam's right." Debbie smacked him on the head with the comb. "Don't turn."

"Watch those nails!" Candy yelled.

"I want to see what Anoushka found."

"I've got the dress! I've got the perfect Shirley Temple dress!" Anoushka held up something short and white with red polka dots.

*Good Lord,* Winston thought. *She can't seriously think I'm going to wear that!*

"Isn't it perfect?" Anoushka demanded. "It's a good thing I brought some of my ice-skating costumes with me or we would have had a hell of a time finding the right dress."

"My middle name must be Lucky," Winston mumbled.

Anoushka grabbed his hand. "Come on!" she ordered. "Let's try this on you."

"Watch out for his hair!" Debbie shouted.

"Wait for me!" Denise Waters charged into the bathroom with a pair of red patent-leather shoes and white ankle socks in her hands.

Winston, almost on his feet, collapsed back onto the chair. He could not let Denise Waters see him in a skating dress. It was bad enough that she was seeing him with his face made up and blond sausage curls covering his head. Denise Waters was possibly the most beautiful girl he'd ever seen. There was no way he was putting on a dress designed for Minnie Mouse in front of her.

"Come on," Anoushka said. "Up!"

Denise winked at him. "I like your knees, Winnie. They're very attractive."

*I'm not going to faint,* Winston told himself.

*I'm not going to be sick to my stomach. I'm going to act like this is fine. Like it's perfectly normal for the most stupendous girl on the continent to compliment my knees.*

Anoushka tugged the dress over his head. "There!" She stepped back, Samantha and Debbie on one side of her, Denise and Candy on the other. "Well? What do you think?"

"Fantastic," Samantha said.

"You look great," said Debbie.

Candy blew him a kiss. "I've always liked guys in polka dots."

Denise put her arms around him. "I think I may have to stand guard over you tonight," she said. "If the psycho really is going to go for a blonde, I sure wouldn't want it to be you."

Isabella flicked her tail. "I don't really know Geoff Gordon," she said as she admired herself in the mirror. "He's one of those guy's guys, if you know what I mean. He's always riding something too fast or gunning something else down, but I guess he's all right." She fiddled with her whiskers. "Anyway, it's only one date, right? And he is a Sigma, so I guess that counts in his favor."

Jessica adjusted her robe with a sigh. "Yeah, I guess so." If she couldn't go to the Halloween dance with the man of her dreams, then she didn't really care if she went with King Kong. Or Geoff Gordon. Although Geoff was cute enough, Jessica's secret feeling was that he had less charisma than a stick insect.

Isabella raised one eyebrow, causing her to look even more like a cat than she already did. "And he isn't Mike McAllery," she added, as though reading Jessica's thoughts. "So that's another five points for him."

"I wish everybody would stop being so down on Mike," Jessica grumbled. "None of you have given him a chance."

Isabella pulled on her paws. "Giving Mike McAllery a chance if you're a woman would be like giving Davy Crockett a chance if you were a bear." Her expression became unusually serious. "I mean it, Jess, I could—"

Jessica jumped up as the phone rang. She didn't want to hear what Isabella thought about Mike. All she wanted to hear was his voice, asking her out, telling her how beautiful she was. She paused for just a second before picking up the receiver, praying that this time it would be him.

"Hello?" She held her breath.

There was the crackle of static and then, from somewhere that sounded very far away, a familiar voice. "Jess? Is that you?"

*"Lila?"* The last letter she'd had from Lila had arrived two days ago, saying she was fine but had been held up because of some business of her mother's and would be back in California within the next two weeks. "Lila, where are you?"

"I'm here." Lila laughed as though someone near her had said something funny. "Here in Italy."

Even though Lila was thousands of miles away and the connection was bad, Jessica could tell something was up.

"But why?" she demanded. "I thought you'd be on your way home by now."

"I thought so too." Lila laughed again. "But I guess I was wrong."

"What do you mean, you *guess* you were wrong? Lila, what's going on?"

The line crackled and Lila giggled. Jessica could just make out another voice, a man's voice, talking close to the phone in Italian.

"Are you ready?" Lila said. "Maybe you should sit down for this, Jess."

"Lila!"

There was another wave of static and then, almost drowning beneath it, Lila's screaming. "I got married, Jess! I got married yesterday!"

Jessica was certain she hadn't heard her right. Her best friend, a girl her own age, couldn't possibly have gotten married. *"What?"* she shrieked. "You did *what* yesterday?"

"I got married, Jess! He's wonderful. He's a count. His name's Tisiano Mond—" She broke off and Jessica could hear the other voice, the Italian voice, again. "I've got to go, Jess, they just announced our plane. We're on our way to Paris."

"But Lila . . ."

"I'll write, Jess, I promise I'll write. As soon as we get back from our honeymoon."

She heard a click and the line went dead. Jessica stood there for several seconds, staring at the receiver, trying to catch her breath, trying to take in what she'd just heard. Her best friend, Lila Fowler, was a married woman. A married woman living in Italy with a count.

"Jess?" Isabella was slipping on her jacket. "Get moving, will you? We're supposed to be meeting the guys downstairs in three minutes."

Jessica didn't move. Lila was flying to Paris on her honeymoon with an Italian count, and she was going to a Halloween dance with a guy who had the foot of a rabbit he'd shot hanging from his rearview mirror. Lila was a real woman now—a real woman with a real man. And Jessica was still a kid going to dances.

"Earth to Jessica!" Isabella boomed. "Let's go!"

A pang ran through her as she realized how much she'd missed Lila. Lila would have been on her side with Mike. She wouldn't have tried to turn Jessica against him; she would have helped her get him.

Slowly, Jessica put down the phone and picked up her bag. "I'm ready," she said. *I am ready,* she thought as she followed Isabella out the door. Ready to get what she wanted, just as Lila had.

# Chapter Eleven

The Xavier Hall gym was draped in jack-o'-lanterns and skull lights and black-and-orange paper chains. Waterfalls of colored cellophane dripped from the ceiling, and ghosts and witches dangled in midair. Celine stood in the doorway like an actress about to take the stage. Although she'd had several invitations to the dance, she'd decided to go by herself. She didn't want some guy who thought he owned her cramping her style.

Across the room, dressed as Count Dracula, she could see William White, looking so handsome and smug that he stood out against the crowd like a moon against a black sky. No, she definitely didn't want anybody getting in her way tonight.

Celine's bracelets jangled as she adjusted one of her thin silk scarves across her breasts. She had chosen her costume with care. She'd wanted to make a statement. She moistened her lips with her tongue and shook out her hair as she slowly began to make her way across the gym. She'd wanted something that would melt every man at the dance, even the cold-blooded Mr. White. She could feel the male eyes following her as she walked, her scarves trailing, her bracelets tinkling, and her movements tempting. A satisfied smile appeared on her beautiful face. That was what she'd wanted, and that was what she'd achieved.

Or almost achieved. Even Celine could see that the look William gave her as she came up to him was not exactly the look of a man helplessly melting with desire.

"Let me guess," he said. "Salomé."

She let one of her scarves fall carelessly across his arm. He was bluffing. Even he couldn't be so immune to her. He was human, wasn't he? He was made of flesh and blood. "How clever of you," she said. "You got it in one."

His eyes moved from her gold sandals to the beads woven through her hair. "Subtlety has never been your strong point, Celine," he said. "Whose head is it you're planning to serve on a platter?"

Celine laughed, brushing against him. "You don't need to worry," she said softly. "I like your head just where it is."

He picked up his glass of punch. "I wasn't worried," he said as he turned away. "You're the last person I'd lose my head over."

She watched her scarf fall from his arm. Did he

really think she would give up that easily? Did he really think he could resist her forever? Celine took a step to follow him, but then she saw Peter Wilbourne III, dressed as a skeleton, coming toward her. Peter might not be William White, but he was handsome and powerful and wealthy. And she could tell from the smile on his face that he appreciated her costume in the way she'd intended.

*You'll do for now,* Celine decided as she looked his way. What William needed was a little competition. A challenge. She knew he was enough like her to want what he thought he couldn't have, to want something that belonged to someone else. Celine looked straight into Peter's eyes. *Yes, you'll do just fine.*

*I should have stayed in the dorm,* Elizabeth decided as she entered the dance behind a clown, a flower, and a box of cornflakes. *I was crazy to come.* She tugged at her costume. In the end she'd decided to dress as Justice. She'd made a scale out of cardboard painted gold and a blindfold from an old white scarf with eyeholes cut in. For the gown, she'd wound herself in a white sheet. She'd thought that it might hide the fact that she was no longer as slender as she used to be, but she had the suspicion that the effect was more like Frosty the Snowman without the hat and scarf.

*You don't have to stay,* she told herself as she hovered at the edge of the dance. *You can just check it out and leave.* Her eyes searched the crowded room. Deep in her heart, she knew exactly why she'd come. She was hoping to see Todd.

"I really am crazy," she mumbled to herself as she pushed her way a little farther into the room. What was the use of running into Todd? He was right: things weren't working between them; they were better off apart. But then she felt someone staring at her, and her heart began to race. *Todd,* she thought. *He's here. He's looking for me, too.*

Unable to stop herself, she turned to see who it was. It was a guy in a black bodysuit and hood, skeletal bones painted on it in pale blue, luminous paint. His black half-mask was hanging around his neck, so she could see he was watching her intensely, but not with yearning or regret; he was watching her with loathing. Elizabeth raised her chin and stared back. She wasn't going to let a creep like Peter Wilbourne III intimidate her.

Swinging her cardboard scales of justice, Elizabeth marched toward a group of girls she recognized from one of her classes. She'd hang out with them for a few minutes, then go home.

When she reached them, however, they were so engrossed in their own conversation that she felt too shy to interrupt. Elizabeth stepped back against the wall, trying to give the impression that she was waiting for someone. Her eyes started scouring the room again. Winston, dressed as Shirley Temple, was doing a tap dance for a bunch of laughing Sigmas. Jessica was in the middle of the room, locked in the embrace of a large guy also dressed as a skeleton. Elizabeth gave her sheet another tug. Jessica, too, was wearing a white sheet, but on her it looked svelte and seductive. Feeling spectacularly unattractive, Elizabeth turned her gaze in the other direction.

*I don't believe it!* Elizabeth stared across the room. The man from the library, the one with the piercing eyes and the cool good looks, really had come as Dracula. But what was even more amazing was that he was talking to Celine. At least, Celine was talking to him. *What could an intelligent guy like that see in her?* Elizabeth wondered.

Very little, apparently. Elizabeth felt a small zing of joy run through her as he suddenly stalked away, leaving Celine standing by herself. Elizabeth just couldn't resist a tiny smile. *That's better,* she thought. The smile grew when Peter Wilbourne materialized beside Celine. *That's much better.* Celine and the Sigma president were a perfect couple. They were both arrogant and they were both stupid. It should give them plenty to talk about.

Elizabeth's eyes sought out Dracula again. "I'm glad you don't like Celine," she whispered to herself. But she didn't ask why.

"Is Elizabeth dancing with that oaf Geoff Gordon?" Mark asked as he handed the gypsy beside him a glass of punch. He frowned. "Talk about going for the wrong person on the rebound.

Geoff Gordon's got to be at least two rungs behind the chimp on the evolutionary ladder."

Enid shook her head. "That's not Elizabeth, that's Jessica." She nodded toward the other side of the room. "That's Elizabeth over there." *By herself,* she added silently, feeling a slight twinge of guilt. "I'd think you'd be able to tell them apart," she teased. "After all, you did spend a whole evening with Jessica."

"Two hours and twenty-six minutes," Mark corrected her. "And two hours and twenty-five of those minutes were spent thinking about you." He slipped his arm around her shoulders. "Anyway, you must admit that their costumes are almost identical. Anybody would have trouble telling them apart."

Enid leaned against him. Even though she didn't want them to, her eyes kept going back to Elizabeth. Enid's life had been so busy and exciting since school began that it had been easy not to think about Elizabeth. But now she couldn't help wondering what had gone wrong. How could so many years of closeness disappear so quickly?

"It's a shame about Elizabeth and Todd, isn't it?" Mark asked, obviously thinking similar thoughts. "From what I understand, they really went through a lot together. They really loved each other." He rested his head on hers. "They had the kind of relationship I could imagine having with . . . with someone like you."

Enid turned to look in his eyes, Elizabeth and her problems fading once again. "Maybe we should dance," she said. "I think this punch is going to your head."

A lean figure, all in black from his boxer's shoes to his knit cap, moved unseen through the night, circling Xavier Hall as silently as a bat. When he reached the rear entrance he stopped, listening.

Tom had chosen his costume carefully. He couldn't risk anything bright or flamboyant, or anything that could be easily spotted in the dark. Tom hadn't come to the Halloween dance to have a good time. He'd come to keep an eye on Elizabeth. Maybe he was crazy, but if there was going to be a beautiful blond victim tonight, he was going to make sure it wasn't her.

Satisfied that there was no one in hiding outside, Tom slipped soundlessly through the door. As soon as he reached the gym, his eyes began to search the crowd for the pale figure in the flowing white robes, but all he seemed to see were skeletons. There were skeletons by the refreshment table. Skeletons by the front door. Skeletons dotted across the dance floor. Tom frowned. *And they're all Sigmas.* Obviously, he wasn't the only one who wanted anonymity tonight.

All at once his eyes caught a flash of white and gold in the center of the room. Tom's stomach knotted and his heart did a double flip. Her back was to him, but there she was, in the arms of one of the Sigma skeletons.

"What's she doing with Gordon the Moron?" Tom muttered. Talk about dicing with death; there was Elizabeth, dancing with it. It was a good thing he wasn't the type to get involved, or he'd just go over there and drag her away from Geoff.

While Tom watched, his heart pounding and his jaw set, the couple turned. "It's not her!" he whispered aloud. He'd made a mistake. That wasn't Elizabeth, that was Jessica. For the first time all evening, Tom smiled. *I knew she was too smart to go out with a dork like that.*

Almost laughing with relief, Tom resumed his search. And then he saw her, standing all alone at the other side of the gym. Tom's heart did another flip. How could he mistake Jessica for her? They might be identical twins, but there was something about Elizabeth that made her stand out from everyone else, even from someone who looked just like her.

Tom stared at the face that seemed to have been burned into his memory. He'd assumed that Elizabeth would have a date tonight and that he'd just watch her from afar. But she clearly didn't. *It's not like I'm trying to pick her up or anything,* Tom told himself as he slowly started to cross the room. *But it'll be a lot easier to keep her safe if I'm right beside her.*

Halfway across the gym, Tom saw something that

made him stop in his tracks. Three skeletons were slipping out one of the exits, and Tom was pretty sure that the one in the lead was Peter Wilbourne. *Now what are they up to?* he wondered, torn between going to Elizabeth and following them.

Whatever the Sigmas were up to, he knew it was trouble. Tom looked around for Danny. If he was going to follow the Sigmas, maybe he should at least have a little moral support.

Suddenly the lights started flickering. A few nervous shrieks rose above the general din. Winston looked at his watch. It was getting close to the bewitching hour, when the psychic had predicted the killer would strike.

"What's the matter, Win?" Bill asked, giving him a playful shove. "You think the psychopath's coming to get you?"

Winston grinned back. "Of course not. I don't believe those stories."

"Well, some people do," Bill said with a laugh as the lights flickered again.

Winston looked toward the far exit. Three guys masked and dressed as skeletons were slipping through the door. A vaguely curious thought raced through Winston's brain. There were quite a few skeletons at the dance—in fact, most of the Sigmas, including Bill, seemed to have come as skeletons.

"That wasn't Peter Wilbourne and his pals leaving, was it?" he asked, hoping he was making it sound like a joke. Peter Wilbourne didn't seem like the type to be scared by a few rumors.

Bill winked. "Maybe."

For the first time Winston seriously wondered if the prediction might come true. After all, if a bunch of macho guys like the Sigmas left because the lights were flickering . . .

"Maybe?" he repeated.

Bill laughed. "Chill out, Win," he said. "It's Halloween, remember? Haven't you ever heard of trick or treat? Maybe the brothers are going to play a little trick on someone."

Winston pushed a curl out of his face, hoping his relief wasn't showing. "Oh, right," he said. "I figured it must be something like that."

Bill put a hand on his shoulder. "Sure you did, Win."

"No, I did, really," Winston protested. Suddenly Bill tightened his grip.

"Do my eyes deceive me?" Bill asked. "Or is the beautiful Anoushka heading our way?"

"Anoushka?" Just when he'd thought it was safe to hang out in public, along came Anoushka to ruin everything. Panic galloped through Winston at an alarming rate. "Where?"

Bill released him. "Right here."

She was dressed as a gunslinger in a black suit, a black cowboy hat, and black cowboy boots. She looked incredible.

"Winnie!" She hurled herself into his arms.

"Don't you think he looks wonderful?" she demanded, turning to Bill. "I was watching him shave the other morning, and I decided he'd make a wonderful girl."

Bill frowned. "Are you two . . . uh . . . together?" he asked, looking from one to the other.

"Sure. We live together." Anoushka started giggling. "Let me tell you," she said, rolling her eyes, "it took hours to get him ready for tonight."

"What?" Bill's smile stayed on Anoushka, but his eyes shifted over to Winston.

"Oops!" Anoushka clapped her hand over her mouth. "I think maybe somebody spiked my punch. I seem to be talking too much."

Bill brought his eyes back to her.

Winston put a hand on Anoushka and tried propelling her away. "You heard her," he said. "She's drunk."

"Oh, please, Winnie, I'm hardly tipsy." She pushed him off. She gave Bill a conspiratorial wink. "Winnie has this big thing about living in Oakley Hall," she told him. "He wants to keep it a secret."

Winston felt his entire blood supply rush to his feet.

Bill turned to him. "*You* live in Oakley?"

As far as Jessica was concerned, the psychic's prediction had come true. There was a psychotic loose at the Halloween dance. Only his weapon wasn't a knife, it was probing hands and a filthy mouth—and he happened to be her date.

"You know what I like best about you, Jessie?" Geoff's voice was thick and low in her ear.

Jessica tried to pull away, but he was holding her tightly.

"Your body." His hand slid down her back again, trying to find a spot not protected by folds of sheet. "That was the first thing I noticed about you, that body."

She reached for his hand and wrapped her own around it. "The first thing I noticed about you is that your ears are very close together," she whispered back. He wasn't listening.

"Not that you can see much of your body in that costume," he was saying. "What are you supposed to be, some Greek god or something?"

"Or something," Jessica mumbled, willing the music to end. At least she had a good idea now of what Penelope had to put up with while she waited for Odysseus to come home: dozens of Geoff Gordons trying to get her to dance too close.

"You know what you should've come as?" His voice was husky. "You should've come as a harem girl. You know, one of those belly dancers? You would have looked great."

*And you should have come as Jack the Ripper,* Jessica thought. Maybe she could say she was going to the ladies' room and sneak back to her room. She'd be better off sitting by herself in the dorm watching some Halloween horror movie than being here with this goon, living a Halloween horror of her own.

His tongue, a fat, sluglike thing, started twisting its way into her ear. "Why don't we go somewhere you could take that stupid costume off?" he half whispered, half moaned.

This time, by applying a little discreet pressure with her knee, Jessica managed to put a few inches between them. "I don't want to go. I want to stay here." She pressed her arms against his chest.

"But I don't." The music stopped, but instead of stepping back he put his hand flat on the base of her spine. "I want to go somewhere and take that sheet off you." His tongue darted for her ear, but she dodged it.

Jessica's temper finally exploded. *I want to go somewhere and take that sheet off you? Was he kidding?* This time she gave him such a fast, hard shove that he lost his balance and staggered backward a few steps. "I'm not going anywhere with you," she informed him. "I wouldn't go anywhere with you if you were the last guy on the planet."

He lunged forward, grabbing her wrist hard. "Oh yes, you are," he leered. "And you're going now. I'm tired of this stupid dance. I want to have a private party. Just you and me."

She tried to free her hand, but he was twisting the skin so hard that it hurt. "You can have your private party by yourself," she hissed. "How clear can I make it? I don't want to have anything to do with you."

The music started up again, and his arm wrapped around her like the tentacle of an octopus. "I don't care what you want. You came out with me, and you're leaving with me." He pushed against her. "You've been leading me on all night, Jessie. You can't stop now."

His mouth was to her neck, which meant that her mouth was to his neck. But she wasn't going to waste her breath telling him again that her name was Jessica, not Jessie. Instead, she bit him as hard as she could. With a cry of pain he released her, and she started pushing her way through the crowd.

He was right on her heels. "So you like to fight, do you?" he asked, grabbing her from behind. "I like a girl who likes to fight. Let's go outside where we can really get down to it." Holding her so she could barely breathe, he started steering her toward the exit.

Suddenly Jessica was really frightened. Once he got her away from the dance, she would have no chance of escape. She searched desperately for a face she knew. Or even a face she didn't know. Why was there never a knife-wielding psychopath around when you really wanted one?

Geoff shoved her out the door, into the lobby of the gym, mumbling obscenities all the while, his hand trying to find a way into her sheet.

She would scream, that's what she'd do. She'd start screaming like crazy. There were enough people milling around that someone would hear her and realize she wasn't just fooling around. The closer they got to the front doors, the more panicked she felt.

Jessica opened her mouth to let out a wail, but suddenly Geoff let go.

"I don't think she really wants to go with you," a deep, strong voice said right behind her.

Jessica swung around. Danny Wyatt was standing beside Geoff, holding him by the arm.

Geoff pulled himself free. "It's none of your business, Wyatt." He smiled slyly. "We're just having a little lover's argument." The slyness eased into menace. "If you know what's good for you, you'll just go back to whatever hole you crawled out of and leave me and Jessie alone."

Danny looked at Jessica. "Is that true, Jess? Do you want me to go away, or is this guy giving you a hard time?"

Jessica moved toward Danny. "He's giving me a hard time, Danny. He's—"

"Don't listen to her . . ."

Geoff made a grab for Jessica, but Danny stepped between them.

"Jessica doesn't want to go with you, Gordon," he said calmly. "So maybe you should leave."

"Don't let him talk to you like that," said another voice from the side.

Jessica looked around, her panic rising again. She'd been so focused on Geoff and Danny that she hadn't noticed they'd been joined by several other skeletons. She looked around at the faces, expecting to see Peter Wilbourne's, but didn't.

"Don't worry about Danny," another skeleton said. "He's not going to do anything."

Danny eyed them uneasily. Jessica studied the side of his face. It was fear that she saw there, but somehow it wasn't the fear of getting hurt in a fight. It was something worse.

She touched his back. "Let's just go, Danny."

Danny nodded. "I'm taking Jessica home now," he said quietly. "You and your friends can just step aside."

The Sigmas started laughing. "Oooh. You're scaring us."

Jessica slid her hand into Danny's.

The punch was so sudden that Danny staggered back, losing his grip on her.

Jessica screamed.

The skeletons laughed again.

This time, Geoff managed to get hold of Jessica and yanked her to his chest. "I'm warning you, black boy," he hissed. "If you don't mind your own business, you're really going to be sorry."

One of the Sigmas gave Danny a shove from the side. "Wyatt's not black, he's yellow."

Jessica couldn't look into Danny's eyes because she was afraid of what she would see there, so she looked at his hands instead. They were so tightly clenched his knuckles were white. He was going to back down again, she could sense it. The Sigmas could sense it too.

Geoff patted her hip. "Let's get out of here, baby." He smiled at Danny. "I think your savior would rather go back to his room and play solitaire."

Jessica looked at Danny, her eyes filled with tears.

"Let her go," Danny said.

One of the Sigmas reached out and ruffled his hair. "You're scaring us," he taunted.

"Let her go."

The Sigmas just laughed.

Winston stared back at Bill, every cell in his body as frozen as a bar of ice cream. It was all over. It was done. He was back to being Winston the loser, the clown. In about ten minutes, as soon as Bill stopped laughing and went back to his friends, the Sigmas would all know that Winston Egbert lived in a female dorm with a bunch of girls who borrowed his stuff and called him Winnie.

"You live in Oakley?" Bill asked again.

Winston nodded, waiting for the laughter. *Come on, Bill. Let's get it over with.*

It took several seconds for Winston to realize that Bill wasn't laughing. He wasn't even smiling.

"Winston," Bill prodded, "is Anoushka saying that *you* live in Oakley Hall with two hundred girls?"

Winston looked up in astonishment. The tone in Bill's voice wasn't ridicule, it was awe. And the look on his face wasn't mocking, either. The look on his face was pure envy.

Winston stood up tall. Suddenly he had an incredible, wonderful realization. The other guys wouldn't think he was a sissy because his dorm-mates shaved their legs and rarely played contact sports. They would think he was as lucky as a fox in a henhouse. Why hadn't he thought of this?

Winston slipped a companionable arm around Anoushka and smiled. "A hundred ninety-eight, actually, Bill." He winked. "Not that I've had the time to count them all personally, of course."

Tom stopped abruptly in the lobby. He'd found the Sigmas. A bunch of them anyway. And he'd found Danny, too. He'd walked in upon a scene so charged he could feel the violence in the air. Geoff Gordon held Jessica Wakefield by the wrist, and he and his fellow Sigmas surrounded Danny.

"Danny!" he heard Jessica cry as the Sigmas closed in. "Oh, God!"

Tom felt his body tense, poised for a fight. He knew this could get ugly. They weren't just threatening Danny this time. He studied Danny's face and saw there was a strange look of calm.

And then Danny's face changed. Before Tom knew what had happened, Danny had hauled off and punched Geoff with such force that Geoff staggered back against the wall and fell to the ground.

The other Sigmas were even more surprised

than Tom was. They seemed to be frozen. Danny, ready to strike. "Does anybody have anything else they'd like to say to me?"

Nobody did.

He turned to leave, giving a last look at Geoff, who was getting shakily to his feet, his nose and mouth already grotesquely swollen. "Don't mess with me, man. Ever."

Danny spotted Tom at the door. Their eyes met and Danny just shrugged. "It's not that those morons are worth fighting," Danny explained, as the two of them walked out into the cool night. He smiled a small, crooked smile. "But if my brother saw the way they were messing with me, he'd take them all himself. And the man can't even walk."

Jessica knew she should stop and thank Danny, but all she really wanted was to get away from the dance and Xavier Hall as quickly as she could. She fled, not even bothering to try to hide her tears.

Just as she burst through the doors of Xavier and into the black night, she thought she heard someone whispering urgently, but then the night was silent again.

Looking neither left nor right, Jessica ran down the path that led to the dark parking lot. At the bottom she stopped, thinking she heard someone talking again. "Hello? Is somebody there?" The only answer was the rustling of the wind through the trees.

Out of the corner of her eye, Jessica thought she saw something move in the bushes.

"Elizabeth," she heard a voice hiss, so low it was almost inaudible.

"Who's there?" she demanded, trying to keep her voice from shaking. She peered into the dark. "I know someone's there," she bluffed. "I—"

The arm was around her neck, choking off her air before she knew what had happened—before she had a chance to scream.

Elizabeth looked at her watch again, trying to pretend she hadn't been standing against this wall, completely alone, for the past hour.

Why had she ever come to this dance? Just because a few hours of working at the TV station had made her forget how awful things really were? Just because she thought Tom Watts would be here and they'd be able to talk and joke the way they did at the studio? Just because, way at the back of her mind, she'd half hoped that with everyone in disguise she might lose some of her inhibitions, that it might be possible to patch things up with Enid, or Jessica, or even Todd?

Well, she'd been wrong. Neither Enid nor Jessica had given any sign that they saw her, even though she'd tried to catch their attention. Eventually, she'd stopped trying. She didn't need to torture herself by seeing how radiant and happy Enid was with her new boyfriend. And as for Todd, neither he nor Tom Watts seemed to have come to the dance at all.

It was time to give up. Elizabeth moved toward the exit.

And that was when she saw him. It was a sight that chilled her to the bone. Todd was deep in a kiss with a willowy redhead. A girl named Lauren Hill, who Elizabeth recognized from her writing class. They were oblivious to the party around them—and anyone who might be watching them.

For a second Elizabeth felt nothing, and then it was as though a herd of cattle had stampeded through her heart. Throwing her paper scales to the ground, she rushed toward the exit.

*I hate college. I hate it here. I wish I'd never come.* Her eyes flooded with tears as she pushed her way across the crowded gym. *I just want to go home.*

"Well, what have we here?" a high, threatening voice demanded. "Could this possibly be the blonde of my dreams?"

Jessica struggled fruitlessly against him. "Let go!" she gasped. "Let me go!"

His laugh was high and threatening too. "Oh, I don't think so. I don't think that will be possible. First I need to teach you a little lesson about respect."

She thought she saw the glint of steel in the hand that wasn't pressed around her throat. *Oh, God. It was him, the psychopath!* The psychic's prediction had been true after all.

"Please . . ." she begged, almost speechless with terror. "Please, I—"

"Blondes are so troublesome, aren't they?" he cackled. "And you're the most troublesome of all." He tightened his grip.

"Elizabeth! Elizabeth, wait!"

At the sound of Tom's voice, Elizabeth started running faster. The sight of Todd kissing someone else had brought all the loneliness and misery she'd felt in these first disastrous weeks of college right to the surface. Her heart lay in shreds.

She didn't want to talk to Tom now. She didn't want anyone to come near her. She wanted to be alone, in the dark, where she could cry herself into a blank, numb sleep. She threw her weight against the heavy exit door and came out into the cold, black night.

"Elizabeth!" His grip was so strong and so sudden that she had to stop. "Elizabeth, please. I don't think you should go out there by yourself."

Keeping her back to him, she tried to shake herself free. "Tom, don't. I—I have to get out of here."

"Just let me walk you back to your dorm. I just want to make sure that you're safe."

Elizabeth broke free, walking away from him as quickly as she could, her white robe flapping around her ankles. "I'll be fine, Tom. I can get across campus on my own."

"Listen to me for a minute, will you? I'm worried the Sigmas are up to something. It's no secret that Peter Wilbourne's had it in for you since the night of the Theta party. He's not the kind of guy to forgive and forget."

How ironic life was. Her best friend, her sister, and the boy she thought was her one true love hadn't given her a thought in weeks, and here was a virtual stranger worrying about her. The odd thing was that instead of making her feel better, it made her feel worse. Instead of making her feel gratitude, it made her feel even sadder.

"I have to go," she gasped, trying to keep her voice from breaking.

Tom grabbed her shoulders and held her. He looked into her face, and she saw more compassion and care in his eyes than she had seen since she got to college. "Please, Elizabeth, tell me what's wrong. I want to . . . I—I—"

The tears were about to come. And when they did, she knew she wouldn't be able to stop them. They'd go on forever. She broke away. "Please just leave me alone."

Elizabeth ran as fast as she could. All the way back to Dickenson Hall and room 28, tears streaming down her cheeks, her chest heaving.

At the entrance to the dorm, she turned back. She heard a rustling noise and saw a figure like a shadow disappearing into the trees. It was Tom. He had followed her all the way home to make sure she was safe.

She called out her thanks in a shaky voice, but he was already gone.

Jessica tried to scream, but the hand over her mouth muffled the sound. *Please. Oh, God, somebody help me.* Her terror had made her body numb.

And then she heard another voice. A calm, confident voice. "Leave her alone, you bastard."

Jessica felt as though she were being hurled from a nightmare to a dream. Maybe terror was making her hallucinate. Maybe he'd already killed her and this was the afterworld. Because she was sure that was Michael McAllery's voice. She'd recognize it anywhere. There couldn't be two men in the world who sounded like that.

The grip around her neck tightened, and she felt herself being dragged into the woods. *Michael! Is it you?*

Suddenly her attacker staggered backward as Mike pulled him off her. It broke the spell of Jessica's fear. She kicked back at her attacker as hard as she could and freed herself of the arm around her neck. She watched as Mike pulled the man in the ski mask to face him and punched him so hard he fell backward to the ground.

Jessica was feeling so many conflicting emotions, from shock and relief to hatred and love, that she couldn't think to speak, but her heart was shouting *Mike! It really is you!*

She wasn't dead and she wasn't hallucinating.

She was alive and Michael McAllery had come to her rescue, just as he had in her dreams.

"Don't touch her again or I will kill you," Michael said calmly. "And tell that to your buddies out there in the bushes." He stepped back slightly, his handsome face in an easy smile.

And suddenly Jessica felt Michael's arms around her, holding her close as he led her down the path back into the light. "It's all right," he kept whispering in her ear. "I'm here. Nobody's ever going to hurt you again."

Jessica wiped tears from her eyes, the terror in her heart replaced by joy. She wrapped her arms around him.

If she'd had any doubts about why she'd come to college, they were gone now. This was why: this man, this moment; the future they promised.

"Come on, Jess." Mike brushed the hair back from her face. "Let's get out of here. Let's go home."

She closed her eyes as the lips she'd been dreaming of for so long touched hers at last. *This is it*, she thought. *This is my destiny.*